THANKS FOR THE LOVE

Thankful Series Book One: A Novella

MELISSA BALDWIN

Also by Melissa Baldwin

COZY MYSTERY

Poison in Paradise: a tropical romantic mystery

Movie Scripts & Madness (The Madness and Murder Mysteries #1)

Room Service & Murder (The Madness and Murder Mysteries #2)

∾

ROMANTIC COMEDY & CHICK LIT

It Could Happen: A Romantic Comedy

Friends ForNever: A Romantic Comedy

Thanks for the Love: A Novella (Thankful #1)

Thanks for the Memories (Thankful #2)

Thanks for the Friendship (Thankful #3)

Love and Ohana Drama (Twist of Fate #1

Fate and Blind Dates (Twist of Fate #2)

Glances and Taking Chances (Twist of Fate #3)

On the Road to Love (Love in the City #1)

All You Need is Love (Love in the City #2)

From Runway to Love (Love in the City #3)

Pushing Up Daisies Collection (Love in the City short story)

One Way Ticket (written with Kate O'Keeffe)

Fall Into Magic (Seasons of Summer #1)

ISBN: 9798717442015

❦ Created with Vellum

I dedicate this book to the fantastic ladies I worked with on the Love in the City Boxset. Congrats to my fellow USA Today Bestselling Authors! We did it!

Chapter One

*W*elcome to Miami, *bienvenidos*. The lyrics of Will Smith's hit song begin running through my mind along with the image of the Fresh Prince of Bel-Air dancing on the white sands of South Beach. Who doesn't love that song? Yes, it's from the 90s, but its important message still rings true—take a vacation to Miami or in my case, pack up and move there.

My best friend (correction: former best friend) and I listened to it over and over again while planning girls' trips and talking about our future hopes and dreams. Oh, the irony that I'm here right now.

I, Gabby Marshall, am officially a resident of the Magic City. I actually had no idea Miami had a nickname until a few days ago. Who knew?

As I drive over the MacArthur Causeway with the sparkling blue water below me, I think about how I ended up here. It hasn't been an easy road, and it still makes me nauseated thinking about starting my life over. A new city, new friends, a new job—I know there will be difficult days, but I'm up for the challenge. I have to keep reminding myself that change is good and now I have a blank canvas in front of me, blah-blah-blah. And despite my reasons, it was super brave of me to walk away from everything I've ever known. This just proves even I can do hard things.

I pull straight into a parking spot directly in front of Fun in the Sun Realty and exhale loudly.

I made it.

Truth be told, I arrived extra early on purpose so I wouldn't have to parallel park. This may sound ridiculous, but I'm absolutely terrified of parallel parking. I'm talking hyperventilating, sweating, panic-attack-inducing afraid.

Some people are afraid of small spaces or heights, but not me. Just the idea of trying to squeeze myself in between two other cars makes me want to turn in my driver's license and never get behind the wheel again. As silly as it sounds, I'd rather jump out of a plane and float down to the office every day.

On a positive note, I'll probably never be late. I consider it a win-win. I mean I could always park a few blocks away in the garage, but then I'd be a sweaty mess by the time I walked through the front door of the agency. I'm very familiar with the Florida humidity, having grown up in Orlando, and the climate in Miami isn't much different, other than the breeze that comes off the ocean. My new office is two blocks from the beach, which was a huge selling point when I made the decision to pack up my life and get out of Orlando. The hardest part was leaving behind a thriving clientele and years of working for the same company, but I'm hoping my knowledge and experience follow me here and I have just as much success.

When I step inside Fun in the Sun Realty, I'm instantly reminded why I took this leap of faith. The laidback beach vibe of the agency is invigorating, and the sunshine streaming in through the wall-to-wall windows is exactly what I need to motivate me.

"Gabby, welcome," Elizabeth calls from her office. She stands up from her chair and comes out to greet me with a hug. Her long blonde hair is full of loose waves, and she's wearing a short white blazer over a pair of skintight black and white striped pants, and black stilettos. She's also wearing a chunky black and white necklace which is almost as big as her neck. It looks like it might be choking her, but we all make sacrifices for fashion.

Elizabeth is the owner of Fun in the Sun, and we're technically family. Well—sort of. She's my sister-in-law's sister, so I'm not sure what that makes us to each other. Is there such a thing as a sister once removed or something like that?

Regardless, I owe her a lot. When my life fell apart, my sister-in-law Nikki reached out to Elizabeth and asked her if she had any open positions at her real estate agency. From that moment, everything fell into place seamlessly. Not only did she offer me a position, she also informed me that one of her other agents was looking for roommates. I'm still not sure if she was hiring anyone. It's very possible she took pity on me and gave me a job at her sister's pleading.

Maybe I'll ask her someday or maybe not. The reasons don't matter now because I'm here.

Elizabeth is talking a mile a minute, and I'm trying to keep up in between zoning out. She leads me to a desk near the back of the office. There's a new laptop and a tumbler with *Fun in the Sun* printed on it waiting for me.

Unfortunately, the desk isn't next to a window. Being the new girl in town, I can't exactly expect a red carpet leading to the best seat in the house. Even if the owner and I are sort of family, I still need to prove myself, and I intend to.

"The laptop is ready to go," Elizabeth says. "Let me know if you have any questions, and I look forward to seeing you first thing tomorrow morning."

Her phone buzzes on cue, and she rushes back to her office.

My head is still spinning, but in a good way. Tomorrow is my first official day, so I'm glad I have this time to become familiar with my surroundings and get the house keys from my new roommate.

I'm about to sit down at my desk when the front door flies open and Lila saunters in. She has her earbuds in, and she's balancing a massive Louis Vuitton bag and a venti Starbucks cup.

"Enrique, love, of course I want to see you."

She waves as soon as she sees me.

Lila reminds me of that girl in high school that everyone wanted to be friends with. She exudes confidence and class, and her style is on point. She's wearing a long turquoise maxi dress and gold gladiator sandals that lace up her legs. Her black hair is pulled up into a bun on top of her head, and her makeup is so perfect she could teach a tutorial on YouTube. The interesting thing is that I've actually only met Lila once for about five minutes. When I came down here to meet with

Elizabeth, I ran into her right before she was rushing out the door to catch a plane to the Bahamas. She sent me a rental contract, and we agreed to everything via email. I haven't even seen her house in person, but the pictures she sent are amazing.

"Enrique, I promise," she continues as she sets her stuff on a desk in front of one of the glass windows.

I have a feeling she's trying to let poor Enrique down easily.

The house I'm moving in to actually belongs to her parents. Apparently, they were about to put it on the market and she stopped them. She told me the idea of selling her childhood home freaked her out, so she walked away from her beach front condo to move back into the house. It's a sweet story, and she must be pretty sentimental to still be attached to it. My parents have lived in several different homes since I was a child, so I don't have that kind of connection to where they currently live.

"Yes, we will catch up very soon," she insists. "My new roommate is here, so I have to dash."

She sighs as she ends the call and places her phone down on the desk.

"Welcome to the jungle, roomie. You're going to love it here."

I let out a nervous laugh. *The jungle?* I'm not sure I like the sound of that.

"You didn't have to cut your conversation short on my behalf."

She waves her hand. "Oh please, you gave me a great excuse to get off the phone. Enrique is sweet, but he gets a little pushy. I've made it clear that we aren't exclusive. You'd think he'd get the picture by now, right?"

I nod. Although I've barely had any interaction with Lila, so of course I don't know anything about her personal life.

"Anyway, let's get to the important stuff. I have some goodies for you." She begins digging around in her bag.

"Here are your house keys, the gate card, and the garage door opener. I already texted you all the codes, so you should be good to go."

A rush of excitement takes over, making me forget about the jungle comment.

"Thank you so much. I can't wait to see the house."

"Oh, that reminds me, I have great news," she continues. "I found us another roommate. Her name is Reagan, and we met at Pilates class. She's from Iowa or Indiana, or one of those places where it's cold all the time."

I force a smile even though my stomach is twisting into knots. I'm really stepping out of my comfort zone—moving in with not one, but two complete strangers.

"I think you'll really like her. She's super nice and works for one of the big hotel chains."

How does she know I'll like her? She barely knows me.

"I look forward to meeting her," I say. But at the same time, I'm thinking about what it'll be like living with two girls I've never spent any time with.

Lila continues spouting off information about the guards at the gates, the lawn care company, and the housekeepers that come in every other week. I should probably be writing everything down, but before I have a chance her phone rings, making her squeal. "I'm sorry. This is a potential client I've been waiting on."

She answers, and I can't help but listen as she works her magic. She's basically selling a two million-dollar listing right before my eyes. Damn, and I thought I was good. I have no doubt she's earned her spot here at Fun in the Sun Realty. It makes me eager to get started and build a name for myself in Miami.

I scan my card at the gate to my new neighborhood, waving to the guard like I know what I'm doing. As I drive slowly down the street, I take in my surroundings. The manicured lawns are full of tall palm trees and bright tropical flowers. It won't be hard getting used to this drive every day.

My GPS directs me to make several turns and leads me to a grand, cream-colored, sprawling house with a brown spanish tile roof. I pull into the wide circular driveway and park directly in front of two massive glass front doors. I slowly get out of the car and stare up at my new home. So far so good.

As soon as I step through the door, I get excited. The layout is an open concept with tall cathedral ceilings and lots of windows. This is a definite upgrade from my apartment back in Orlando. Don't get me wrong, it was lovely, but nothing like this. Now I can understand why Lila didn't want her parents to part with this house.

I follow her directions and walk toward the left side of the house. I'm pleasantly surprised when I see my room. It's open and spacious with a bay window overlooking the large backyard. There's a pink gift bag sitting on the bed with an envelope leaning against it. Inside I find a large box of Godiva chocolates and a gift card to Trader Joe's. I can't think of a better welcome gift.

After setting my bag down, I wander through the house. It's actually the perfect setup for living with multiple people. The living spaces are all located in the center of the house, with the bedrooms in opposite corners, each with their own bathroom. The private bathroom was a huge selling point for me. The last thing I wanted was to have to share a bathroom with someone I didn't know. That's a recipe for disaster.

The kitchen might be my favorite room in the entire house. There are large beams running across the ceiling, and a huge island in the middle with barstools all around it. It's the perfect space for entertaining. Most party guests congregate in the kitchen anyway. I look in both the fridge and the pantry—Lila has some staples, but I definitely need to make a run to the grocery store today. As much as I love pickles, Cheez-Its, and almonds, I need more sustenance.

I continue my tour, peeking out the french doors at the backyard. The pictures Lila sent definitely didn't do it justice, and it only confirms that I made the right decision to move in here. The resort-style pool is inviting with waterfalls cascading off the rock formations. Next to the pool is an outdoor kitchen with plenty of seating to entertain. Just beyond the pool area are two hammocks hanging between tall palms. I practically race through the yard on my way to one of them. What is it about hammocks that make them so fun?

I sit down in the one with plenty of shade and try to balance myself as I stretch out it. The soft breeze begins to rock the hammock, and I exhale slowly. For a second it almost feels like I could be at a resort in the Caribbean instead of in a neighborhood in a Miami suburb.

"This is perfect," I say out loud.

"Hey, there," a deep voice calls, causing me to shoot up from my position. Unfortunately, I move too quickly and start to lose my balance. As much as I try to hang on to the ropes, I'm unsuccessful.

I begin tipping despite my desperate efforts to stay on, and I hit the ground, hard. Upon impact pain shoots through my left hand, and I wail in agony.

Chapter Two

"*A*re you okay?" a male voice shouts.

I don't know whether to be more worried about the pain pulsing through my arm or the fact that there's a strange man somewhere in my backyard.

All of a sudden, my mother's voice plays in my mind, lecturing me about the dangers of moving to this city. I don't want to have to call her and tell her she was right. I can't even count the number of hours she spent trying to talk me out of it. I appreciate that she wanted me to stay near family, but I still don't know why she didn't understand my reasons for leaving. She knew the hell I went through.

I'm starting to feel a bit nauseated. I don't think I hit my head, but the whole thing happened so fast.

"Hey, don't move yet," he says. I glance up, but the sun is so bright I can't see the stranger's face.

"Stay here. I'll grab you some ice."

Before I have a chance to say anything, he takes off inside Lila's house. *What's happening?* Some random guy just appears out of nowhere, and I let him waltz into my new home like he owns the place. My mind starts spinning with worst-case scenarios, thanks to my mother's wild paranoia. I don't even have my phone with me. It totally figures that the one time I don't have that damn thing glued to my body would be the time I'd actually need it most.

Before I have a chance to make a run for it, the man returns with a bag of ice.

"What hurts?" he asks. "I'm so sorry. I just wanted to say hi, and the next thing I know you were falling."

When I finally get a good look at his face, I let out a gasp. And not in a bad way. I certainly didn't expect him to look—well, like he does. I take in his black wavy hair, grey eyes, and structured jawline. I guess I've officially met a handsome stranger—in my backyard. *Gah, what the hell is wrong with me?*

"I think it's my hand or my wrist," I mutter. Now that I've seen what he looks like, I'm not sure which is worse—the pain or the humiliation.

He gently takes my hand in his and starts giving me instructions. I wiggle my fingers and wince as he presses a few spots in my wrist.

"I think you need to get this checked out."

I nod absently.

My mind is spinning right now. I've only been in town for a few hours, and I have no idea where to find an urgent care or hospital. So much for my plans to spend the rest of my day getting settled.

"How do you know the Barlows?" he asks.

Barlows?

Oh wait, Lila's last name is Barlow.

"I actually just moved here," I say. "But shouldn't I be asking you the same thing? Who are you, and what are you doing in the Barlows' backyard?"

He gives me a sheepish grin. "I live next door."

He points to the house on the right. There's a half stone wall that separates the property, but the layout looks somewhat similar from what I can see.

"So, you were watching me?" I ask. "That's not creepy at all."

All the color drains from his face.

"Ugh. When you put it like that, it really does sound bad."

I should probably be uncomfortable right now, but I'm not at all.

"Just so you know, I promise I wasn't watching you," he insists. "I was sitting on my patio working, and I saw you come outside. I waved, but I guess you didn't see me."

It's totally possible. I must have been so enamored with the resort-style backyard and the hammock that I didn't notice him.

"I'm Theo, by the way. My family has lived next door for years—you're welcome to do a background check."

A feeling of relief washes over me, although just because he's my new neighbor doesn't mean I should completely let my guard down. I barely know Lila, much less her neighbor.

"I'm Gabby."

He flashes me brilliant smile. "It's nice to meet you. I only wish it were under different circumstances."

I catch myself staring at his face again. He's really handsome. *Maybe I did hit my head?*

"It's nice to meet you." I'm still in such a daze, trying to make sense of my fall and Theo being here.

"Anyway, since it was my fault you fell, please let me take you to urgent care. There's one not too far from here."

First, he shows up in my backyard. Now he wants me to get into a car with him. Should I be worried?

"That's nice of you, but I think I'm okay to drive myself."

As I start to stand up, he jumps to his feet to help me.

"Are you sure? Do you know your way around here?"

I chew on my lower lip.

"That's what I thought. I'll meet you out front in ten minutes."

Before I have a chance to say anything, he rushes away and disappears between the houses.

I'm so confused. One minute I'm soaking up the beauty of my new home, and the next I'm injured and getting into a car with a handsome stranger—neighbor.

He's right though—I have no idea where to go, and my wrist really hurts. I could always call an Uber, but isn't that the same thing? I wouldn't know a random Uber driver any more than Theo.

I hurry inside to find my phone. While I wait for Lila to answer, I hold the bag of ice on my wrist.

"Hey," she answers. "What do you think of the house? Are you finding your way around?"

The house is the last thing on my mind at the moment.

"Oh, yes it's beautiful," I say. "And thank you for the sweet welcome gift."

"You're welcome," she says.

I clear my throat. "So, something interesting just happened, and I met your neighbor."

"Really? Which one?

"His name is Theo."

"Theo Jorgenson, ugh." A detect a hint of disgust in her voice, and that's not the reaction I was hoping for.

"That doesn't sound good. Is he trouble?"

She laughs. "No, but I can't stand him. His family has lived next door for forever."

My mind immediately wanders to why she doesn't like him. He was really nice to me—although he did startle me, which made me fall.

"I did hear that he was planning to sell the house, so maybe that's why he's there."

I sit down on the edge of the bed and tell her about my little hammock mishap and how Theo offered to give me a ride.

"I can come get you if you need me to," she says. "I'm waiting on a call, but I can always do that from the car."

The last thing I want is to interfere with Lila's day. I don't want her thinking I'm high maintenance before we even start living together.

I assure her that I'm fine before getting off the phone. Theo is probably waiting for me outside. I glance at my wrist which is now swollen.

I knew this move was going to be an adventure, but I certainly didn't expect it to start like this. I sigh. Here goes nothing.

When I walk outside, there's a sleek black Tesla sitting in front of the house. Theo gets out of the car and meets me at the passenger side to open the door. Okay, so on top of being extremely good-looking, he scores a few points in the gentleman department.

As soon as I'm inside, I'm met with an intoxicating smell of new leather and delicious men's cologne.

"Nice car."

"Thank you," he says, running his hand over the dashboard fondly. It's obvious that he's very proud of it. I wouldn't even be surprised if he's named it. I know a few guys who have named their cars.

A few seconds later, he peels out of the driveway in true show-off flare. I expected nothing less.

"How's your wrist feeling?"

I'm still carefully cradling my arm, but at least the ice has made the pain subside for now. I'm silently praying that it's not something serious.

"It's actually feeling a little better. I'm sure I could've driven myself."

He nods. "Maybe, but this is the least I can do since it's my fault."

I grow more embarrassed each time I think about it. *Who falls out of a hammock?*

"So, where are you from?" he asks. I appreciate that he's changing the subject from my graceful moment.

"Orlando."

"Orlando is a great city. There's so much to do there."

"Yes. It's a lot of fun."

I look out the window as we drive through this tropical paradise that I now call home.

"So, you grew up here?" I ask, changing the subject. I'm not really prepared to get into a discussion about Orlando or why I left.

"I did, but I just recently moved back."

"Where were you living?" I ask.

"I lived in Dallas for two years and Chicago for the two years before that."

"Oh, nice," I say. "I've never really been a big fan of change, but there is something exhilarating about being in a new city."

"I agree," he says. "And here we are."

We pull up in front of the urgent care, and sure enough there's only parallel parking. I guess it was meant to be that Theo drove me here. I'd be freaking out if I had to squeeze in between two other vehicles with only one hand. Theo effortlessly maneuvers his way into the smallest spot I've ever seen, one that would send me into a state of sheer panic. As soon as he turns off the car, he practically jumps out and races to my door. He either feels really guilty about my unfortunate accident, or he's trying to impress me. Or maybe both.

When we approach the front desk, Theo asks if Dr. Sims is working. Why does it not surprise me that he knows the doctor?

The receptionist hands me a clipboard of forms to fill out, and Theo and I take a seat.

"You know the doctor?" I whisper.

He leans in close enough for me to get a whiff of his cologne. It's the same intoxicating smell from inside his car.

"Yep, Cal is one of my closest friends. That's why I wanted to bring you here."

Cal, huh? Well, I guess VIP treatment isn't such a bad thing, especially since they seem to be pretty busy. I could be here for hours.

I quickly finish filling out the fun medical forms, and I'm called back a few minutes later. Theo naturally follows me to the exam room. I guess it doesn't matter if he's with me, especially since he's friends with Dr. Sims. I mean—it's not like it's an appointment with a gynecologist.

Ew. I cringe at the thought.

A nurse comes in immediately to take my vitals, but her focus seems to be on Theo. I can't say I blame her either. He's not hard on the eyes.

"So, how did you hurt your wrist?" she asks, acknowledging my presence.

Theo and I glance at each other, and he frowns.

"I sort of fell out of a hammock and braced myself with my hand."

Yep, it gets more embarrassing each time I say it out loud.

She makes a few notes on my chart.

"Dr. Sims will probably order some X-rays. He should be right in."

She shoots one last dreamy glance at Theo before she leaves. She couldn't have been more blatantly obvious. Maybe she should talk to Dr. Sims about putting in a good word for her?

"I think you have an admirer," I tease.

He shrugs nonchalantly. "Nah."

He seems completely unfazed by the nurse's obvious attempts to get his attention. Maybe this kind of thing happens to him all the time.

"Seriously, she couldn't take her eyes off you," I exclaim. "I'm shocked she was able to take my vitals."

A few seconds later there's a knock on the door and the doctor pops his head in. That was fast. I'm grateful Theo is here with me, I guess who you know really comes in handy.

"Hello, Gabrielle. I'm Dr. Sims."

Cal Sims is almost as attractive as Theo, with thick dirty blond hair and piercing blue eyes. Miami is certainly not lacking in the men department. Too bad I'm trying to stay clear of them altogether.

He points to Theo and shakes his head. "I should warn you about this guy—although I'm obviously too late."

Theo rolls his eyes and lightly punches Cal on the arm.

"Thanks, man."

Both of them laugh.

"Okay, so I see you fell out of a hammock and landed on your hand. Ouch."

I feel my face getting hot. I can't wait for this day to be over so I don't have to explain this to anyone else. Maybe I should change my story.

"Yes."

"Those hammocks can be a hazard," he says. "How did it happen?"

I'm not sure if he's being sarcastic or not.

I purse my lips and glance at Theo. "It was just an unfortunate accident."

Cal looks at my hand and starts asking me questions. I wince as he applies pressure to a few areas.

"Let's get some pictures and see what's going on in there."

I groan.

"I'm going to step out and check my emails," Theo says. He stares at me for a few seconds before leaving the room with Cal. He seems to be genuinely concerned, which is kind of sweet.

The nurse returns and leads me to the X-ray room. She's definitely not as chatty as she was when Theo was in the room. I wonder if he has that kind of effect on women all the time.

The good news is the pain has subsided a lot. I really want to get this over with and go home. I have so much to do, and this is not how I expected to start my life in Miami.

After taking the X-rays, the nurse leads me back to the exam room and tells me that the doctor will be in after he looks at the images.

I hop onto the table and take my phone out to check my messages. There's one message from my mother with two articles about areas to avoid in Miami. I roll my eyes. I don't know if she will ever get used to the idea of me living here. The other is from my sister-in-law checking in on me.

I'm really grateful for Nikki. When she married my brother, I wasn't sure we'd get along, but she's the person who's been there for me through some of my darkest moments.

A few minutes later there's a knock on the door.

"I have good news," Dr. Sims announces.

My heart begins to beat against the walls of my chest. Moment of truth.

"What is it?"

"The images are showing that it's just a bad sprain. It should heal relatively quickly if you take it easy."

I breathe a sigh of relief. "Thank goodness."

"So that means rest, ice, compress, and anti-inflammatory meds for the pain. I'm sending you with a bandage to keep it immobile for a few days."

"Thank you so much," I say.

"You're welcome," he says. "I'm still going to check in with Theo to make sure you're following orders."

"Oh, I actually don't really know him." I pause when I realize how stupid I sound. "I mean, we just met."

Dr. Sims gives me a curious look. This is really awkward. He's probably wondering why I'm here with Theo if I barely know him.

"Well, in case you're wondering, he's one of the good guys," he says with a gleam in his eye. "We've been friends since high school."

I consider asking him if he knows Lila, but I know he needs to get back to work.

"Thanks for letting me know," I say awkwardly.

"I'd also like you to follow up with your primary care doctor in a few weeks if you have any concerns."

"I actually just moved here, so I don't have a doctor yet."

He nods. "No problem. Just let me know if you need anything in the meantime."

"I will."

"And welcome to Miami."

I smile. "Thank you. It's definitely been eventful."

When I walk back to the waiting room, Theo is typing something on his phone. He stands up as soon as he sees me. "Well?"

I hold up my bandaged wrist.

"It's only a sprain, so you can stop beating yourself up about it."

His shoulders relax immediately.

"I told her that I'd check in with you to make sure she's resting," Dr. Sims calls from the doorway.

Theo nods. "I'll make sure she is."

What? I give him a curious look, and his eyes lock on mine.

After we're in the car for a few minutes, Theo is the first to break the silence.

"I'm so glad your wrist isn't fractured or worse."

I nod. "Me too. That would be an awful welcome present."

"You never told me. What brought you to Miami?" he asks.

I chew on my bottom lip. This is a loaded question. There's the easy answer, which is a new job, and then there's the complicated answer, which is that I ran away from my ex-fiancé and my ex-best friend. This answer would start a whole conversation I don't want to have.

Thankfully before I can answer, our conversation is interrupted by the sound of my phone ringing.

"It's Lila," I announce. "Hey."

"Hi, I just got home. Where are you?"

"We're on our way home from urgent care."

"Oh, are you still with Theo?"

I shoot a side glance at him.

"Yes."

"Oh, I'm sorry. I should've left the office to take you instead of leaving you in the trenches with him."

Wow. She makes it sound like it's torture to be with Theo, and that couldn't be further from the truth. There has to be more to the story of why she doesn't like him.

"Don't worry about it," I tell her. "I'll be home soon."

"Great. Reagan's on her way too."

I totally forgot about Reagan. The hammock incident and meeting Theo have completely thrown me off my game.

"Everything okay?" Theo asks after I end the call.

"Yep. She wanted to check on me."

"I bet she was. Lila Barlow hates me."

I press my lips together. What am I supposed to say to that?

"I don't know if she hates you, but she did tell me that you two didn't get along."

He scoffs. "That's one way of putting it. You know how there are just some people who don't mesh well together? Well, Lila and I are those people."

We pull through the gate of the neighborhood, and Theo waves to the guard.

"That's William. He works the gate during the day. Nicest man you'll ever meet."

I remember Lila telling me about the guards, but that was when she was spouting off information, and I was barely keeping it all straight.

"I really appreciate you taking me to see Dr. Sims. I'd probably still be sitting in a waiting room somewhere."

"It was my pleasure," he says as he pulls in front of Lila's house. "I'm just sorry you had to go in the first place."

He puts the car in park, and neither of us says anything. I should probably go inside but something is keeping me from opening the door.

"Let me know if you need anything while you're getting settled," Theo says, turning toward me. His grey eyes lock on mine as I study the outline of his face.

"I will." I pause. "That reminds me, Lila said she heard you might be selling your house."

The corner of his mouth curls up. "I've thought about it."

This is my chance to casually remind him that I work in real estate. I need to utilize every connection I make.

"Well, please keep me in mind if you don't have a realtor yet."

He smiles. "Definitely. And I'll be happy to pass your information along to friends."

I beam. "That would be amazing. It's going to be a lot of work to build my business, so I'll take all the help I can get."

"Do you have a business card?"

I dig in my bag for one of my cards. "This is an old card, but my cell number is on it."

I finally open the door despite my strange hesitation.

"Gabby."

"Yes." My stomach does a little flip, and I turn around to face him.

"Make sure you rest your hand. I don't want to have to tell your doctor that you aren't following orders."

I frown. "Would you really tell on me?"

He shrugs. "That depends."

"Don't worry. I'll be a good girl," I say playfully.

As soon as the words come out of my mouth, I regret it.

He raises his eyebrows. "It was nice meeting you."

"You too, Theo." I shut the door and walk toward the house. When I turn to wave, Theo is still watching me. He waves one more time and then pulls out of the driveway.

My head is spinning as I try to make sense of our strange interaction. Despite my attraction to Theo, I made a promise to myself that I would steer clear of men for a while. The only thing that's important right now is building my career and getting settled in my new life. Everything else will only complicate things, and that's the last thing I need right now.

Chapter Three

*A*s soon as I walk into the house, Lila greets me with a glass of wine. How does she still look so glamorous in her yoga pants and hoodie? I could be wearing the same clothes and look like I haven't showered in days.

"I'm sure you need this after spending all that time with Theo Jorgenson," she says with a laugh. "And I have plenty more where this came from."

I giggle. "Actually, it wasn't bad. He was really polite and attentive. He drove me to urgent care and even sat with me before I got X-rays."

She makes gagging sounds. "Oh girl, please don't fall for his charm."

I laugh nervously. "Absolutely not. I know better."

"Anyway, welcome home," she says holding her arms out. "Reagan just got here a few minutes ago. She's changing."

Here we go. The three of us are officially beginning our adventure of living under the same roof starting tonight. I take a long sip of wine, hopefully it will calm my nerves.

When I walk into the kitchen, I'm met with a fantastic spread of food including a gorgeous charcuterie tray, fruit, vegetables, and some french pastries.

"This is amazing, Lila," I exclaim. "You didn't have to do this."

She shrugs. "I thought it would be a nice way to spend our first evening getting to know each other."

So far Lila is turning out to be an excellent roommate. First the thoughtful welcome gift, and now all of this food. Not to mention I'm absolutely starving.

"Lila, thank you for the gift," a high-pitched voice says. I turn around to see a petite girl with short blonde hair and big brown eyes.

"Hi. You must be Gabby," she squeals. "I'm Reagan."

You know how sometimes you instantly get a good vibe from people? Reagan is one of those people.

"Hi. It's nice to meet you," I say, giving her a warm smile. "Isn't this house amazing? And look at all of this." I point to the food and reach for a cracker.

"I know. It's totally unexpected," she says, her voice lowering a few octaves. "Oh no, what happened to your wrist?"

Lila hands Reagan a glass of wine.

I sigh. "It's actually really stupid. When I got here earlier today, I was checking out the backyard. Long story short—I fell out of the hammock and broke my fall with my hand."

"Ouch," Reagan says.

"Thankfully, it's only sprained," I add.

"I'm not surprised that happened," Lila interjects. "Anytime Theo is around, there's chaos. He's like a wrecking ball that destroys everything in its path."

"Who's Theo?" Reagan asks before taking a sip of her wine.

"He's the next-door neighbor," I say. "But Lila doesn't like him."

I throw a glance that way. She's nodding her head in agreement.

"You got that right."

"What's wrong with him?" Reagan asks as if she's reading my mind. *I knew I liked her.*

Lila sighs dramatically. "Theo Jorgenson destroyed my life."

Whoa. I knew there was more to the story, but that's quite an accusation. Although now I'm wondering why Theo didn't give me his side of the story.

"The Jorgensons moved here when I was in high school. At first, we didn't have any interaction. We had different friends, and our paths never really crossed. When we were seniors, I started dating one of his friends. Everything was going perfectly until my ex-boyfriend, Brent, came home from college. He stopped over here to talk to me about rekindling our relationship, but I wasn't interested. Anyway, he ended up kissing me right out front, and Theo saw it. The next thing I knew, my relationship was over, and I'm still convinced it was Theo's fault. I'm sure he sabotaged my relationship by telling my boyfriend Cal about me and Brent."

She sighs. "It's been six years, and I've never had those kinds of feelings for anyone else. I was so head over heels in love with Cal."

Both Reagan and I are listening intently until something clicks.

"Wait. Are you talking about Cal Sims as in Dr. Sims?"

Lila stares at me. "Yes, how do you know him?"

I hold up my bandaged wrist.

Her jaw drops, and she puts her hands to her mouth.

"Your wrist. Theo took you to see Cal."

I nod. "He told me they'd been friends since high school. I wondered if you two knew each other."

"Oh, I didn't realize his office was nearby," Lila says. "I actually sent him a friend request on Facebook a while ago, but I don't think he goes online much. Or he just ignored my request."

"Wow, what are the chances that Theo would take you to Cal's office," Reagan exclaims.

Lila is staring off into space like she's a million miles away.

Hmm …

"Just so you know, I have to follow up with Dr. Sims since I don't have a primary physician yet."

She sips her wine and shrugs. "I'm sure Cal Sims is happily attached. Men like him don't stay single for long."

I shrug. "I don't know, but I'm sure I could find out."

"That's a great idea," Reagan agrees.

"We'll see," Lila says nonchalantly. "Anyway, I'd like to make a toast to us. I'm so grateful that you're both here and agreed to move in. It's been a while since I've had roommates, and you've made my decision to leave my condo easier."

Thankfully we drop the subject of Theo and Cal. I'd rather not spend our first evening together talking about men.

Lila shows us photos of her picturesque beach-front condo. I have to say that as amazing as this home is, it would've been difficult for me to walk away from that view.

"I'm so happy you told me my pants were inside out in our Pilates class," Reagan says with a laugh.

"What?" I exclaim.

Reagan tells the story about the first time she and Lila met, and we all laugh hysterically.

"From that moment on we started talking, and I told her I was looking for a new place to live." Reagan says, "I had reached my limit living with my sister and her new husband. By the way, I don't recommend living with newlyweds."

"So, you were obviously meant to put your pants on wrong that day," I suggest.

Reagan giggles. "Exactly."

"What about you, Gabby?" Lila asks. "Why did you decide to come to Miami? I mean, other than to work for Elizabeth."

I sigh. It's not exactly a secret as to why I'm here but it's still raw to talk about.

"Well, long story short, I broke off my engagement when I found my fiancé and my best friend together."

"No," Reagan shouts.

"Stop," Lila demands.

I nod. "Yep. My boyfriend of three years and my best friend of forever had been having an affair for over a year."

"That's terrible," Reagan says.

"So, to answer your question, I'm here because I literally ran away from my problems," I say. "It was the worst five months of my life, and I knew I had to get out of Orlando."

Reagan reaches over and pats me on the back.

"If it's any consolation, you came to the right place to get over that jackass," Lila adds. "I can introduce you to some great men. Especially since your only interaction so far is with Theo Jorgenson."

Theo's handsome face flashes through my mind. I must have a swoony expression on my face because Lila gives me a horrified look.

"No, Gabby," she wails. "Please don't tell me I'm too late. You can't be interested in him already."

I hold up my hands. "Actually, I promised myself that I'd stay far away from men for a while. I'm sure you can understand that I'm a bit jaded at the moment. My career is my number one priority right now."

Lila shakes her head. "You do know that the best way to get over someone is by meeting someone else."

Reagan nods. "Yes, I agree."

I sigh. "Well, that may be the case, but I'm in a good place, and I don't need a man coming in and messing everything up."

"Who said anything about a relationship?" she asks, giving me a wink.

I laugh.

"Anyway, that's enough talk about my disaster of a life," I announce. "Reagan, how long have you lived in Miami?" I remember Lila saying she moved here from a cold climate.

"I've been here about eight months, and I haven't looked back," she says. "I had enough of the miserable winters in Illinois."

"I thought you were from Iowa," Lila says with a giggle. "I knew it started with an I."

"Nope, I was born and raised outside of Chicago. My parents are still in Illinois, but my sister lives down here."

The three of us spend the rest of the evening talking and eating. When I finally lie down in my new room, I think about everything that's already happened since I got to Miami. I have a really good feeling about this place. As difficult as the last few months have been, perhaps I'm exactly where I'm supposed to be.

Chapter Four

I know it'll take some time to get used to my new surroundings, but I didn't expect to be wide awake before the sun rises. I'm a morning person, but this is ridiculous.

After lying in bed thinking about every major life decision I've ever made, I finally decide to get up and make some coffee. I'm running on about four hours of sleep, so I'm sure this will be my first of many cups. It's my first day at Fun in the Sun Realty, and I want to be on top of my game. Falling asleep at my desk isn't the best impression to make.

It's still dark out, so I decide to enjoy my caffeine out on the patio. The morning breeze mixed with the humidity hits my skin as soon as I walk outside. One thing is for sure, I'm definitely steering clear of the hammocks. In fact, I may never sit in one of them again.

I'm about to curl up on one of the chaise lounges when I notice the patio lights come on at Theo's house. I guess I'm not the only crazy one to be up at this hour. My curiosity is piqued when I hear a loud splash, so I tiptoe over toward the stone wall to see if I can catch a glimpse of him.

As I approach the wall, I notice Theo's pool is lit up, and he's swimming laps. My eyes zero in on his back muscles as he makes his way swiftly through the water, and I can't help but be impressed by how fast he's swimming. I can barely dog paddle, while he's doing a super fancy flip off the wall without coming up for air.

I consider saying hi, but I don't want to startle him. He may not be relaxing in a hammock, but the last thing I want is for him to smack his head on the side of the pool.

After several laps he stops and stretches his arms above his head. Just as I'm about to sneak away, I knock my coffee cup over, and hot liquid spills down the side of the wall.

"Crap," I exclaim, louder than I intended.

There isn't much noise at this hour, so of course he hears me. He turns around and looks in my direction. It'd look much worse if I tried to make a run for it, so I wave awkwardly instead.

He lifts himself out of the water effortlessly and makes his way toward me.

He's actually coming over. *Why do I have to be so nosy?*

As he struts toward me, my eyes lower to his ripped torso. *Damn, he looks good.*

"Um—hello," I say. All of a sudden I want to crawl away and hide.

"Good morning, neighbor," he says cheerfully. "You're up early."

I groan. "Not by choice. Being in new places does a number on my sleep habits. Obviously, it's much too early for me to be awake since I can't hold on to my coffee." I point to the lovely mess of brown liquid seeping into the cream-colored stone wall.

"I get it," he agrees. "I struggle the first night or two when I'm traveling. I usually get acclimated just in time to go home."

It suddenly hits me that when I rolled out of bed, I barely looked in the mirror. I try to subtly run my hand through my hair without being too obvious.

Although it's still dark, the sun is beginning to rise. Soon Theo will see me in all my morning glory, and there's nothing I can do about it. At least I'm wearing a cute pair of pajamas and UGG slippers instead of my dad's faded Tampa Bay Bucs shirt that I sleep in sometimes.

"I was sitting outside with my coffee when I saw your light come on, so I was just checking ..."

Ugh. I quickly try to come up with something clever to say, but it's not happening. I've got nothing.

"So, you were watching me swim," he says, giving me a wink. He's made no effort to dry off or put a shirt on. *Not that I'm complaining.*

"No," I lie.

He laughs. "It's okay if you were."

I scowl. "Well, I could the say the same thing about you. Remember this?"

I hold up my hand to remind him of my wrist injury.

"Fair enough. I guess that makes us even now," he teases.

"I guess it does."

I'm trying my best not to stare at the pool water glistening off his bare upper body.

"How's your wrist feeling today?"

I hold out my hand to him. The swelling has gone down quite a bit.

"It's actually feeling better, just sore."

The sun is starting to peek out of the horizon, and light is slowly filling the sky.

"My first Miami sunrise," I say excitedly. "Seeing this makes getting up early worth it."

He nods. "It is pretty amazing. I'm awake at this time every day, but I never take the time to appreciate it."

"Do you swim every morning?"

"Usually. Or I run a few miles."

Of course, he does.

"I should probably let you get back to it then," I say, picking up my now empty coffee cup. "Have a great day."

"Have you had breakfast yet?" he asks.

What?

"No. I haven't had a chance to get any groceries. Lila told me to help myself, but all she has is oatmeal and a box of Lucky Charms."

"Lucky Charms are pretty delicious," he points out. "But not as good as my omelets. Do you want to join me?"

I glance down at my light blue pajamas and slippers. *Is he really asking me to have breakfast with him while I look like this?*

"Um, that's nice of you. But I'm kind of a mess."

He grins. "You look cute—although your hair is doing something funny in the back."

I pat the back of my head, and sure enough my hair is all mangled and sticking up in different directions. I'm not surprised since I think I'm on day three of dry shampoo.

I laugh. "Obviously I didn't expect to see anyone this morning, but just so you know, I brushed my teeth."

Why did I tell him that?

"That's good to know," he says. "Come on over, unless you had your heart set on Lucky Charms."

The crazy thing is I really want to take him up on his invitation, especially after seeing him shirtless, and I do love omelets.

I let out a loud sigh. "Well, since you've already seen me at my worst, why not?"

"Exactly," he teases.

He points to a gate between the houses and meets me on the other side.

I follow him toward the french doors, and on the way, he grabs a towel and wraps it around his waist. He still hasn't made any attempt to cover his upper body. *Is he doing it on purpose?*

"Help yourself to a fresh cup of coffee. I'll be right back."

"Thanks."

I look around Theo's kitchen. It's a similar layout to Lila's, but the appliances look newer. I place my cup down and lean against the marble countertop.

Being here is so surreal. I'm still trying to wrap my head around the last twenty-four hours. I really expected to be busy unpacking and getting settled in my new home. Somehow, I've ended up in my hot neighbor's kitchen for breakfast. I swear, there's never a dull moment in my life.

"Okay, what do you like in your eggs?" Theo asks, dragging me out of my thoughts.

He's now wearing a snug black T-shirt, black Adidas sweatpants, and flip-flops. Honestly, the man could wear a trash bag and he'd still look good.

"I have spinach, tomatoes, mushrooms, cheese, and bell peppers," he calls over his shoulder.

"All of that sounds good to me."

He peers around the refrigerator door and smiles. "Excellent."

I finally get myself a fresh cup of hot coffee and hop onto a barstool.

Theo starts chopping vegetables like a pro.

"Can I help you with anything?" I ask, wrapping my hands around my cup. "I feel bad sitting here while you do all the work."

"Nope, you're my guest," he says. "And I enjoy doing this."

I suddenly feel like I'm watching a show on Food Network. He throws the veggies into a saucepan and starts cracking eggs.

"You're really good at this cooking gig. You look like a pro."

He chuckles. "I got so sick of ordering takeout. I had no choice but to learn."

"I'm an expert at ordering takeout," I say proudly.

I watch Theo continue to move around the kitchen. He places two plates on the counter.

"So, why did you decide to move to Miami?"

I sip my coffee. There's the big question again. He's probably going to regret asking me once he hears the answer.

"Well, my life in Orlando had basically fallen apart, and I was in a really dark place. When I was offered a job here, I knew I had to go for it because it was my chance to get away."

He's moved to the stove, and I continue watching him work while we talk. He obviously knows what he's doing. I've tried to make omelets on several occasions, but they never seem to turn out. I usually give up and scramble them.

"If you don't mind me asking, how did your life fall apart?" he asks. "Sorry. You don't have to tell me …"

I exhale loudly. There's no reason not to tell him what happened back in Orlando. As difficult as it was, it's part of my life, and maybe sharing it will help me continue to heal.

"I was planning my dream wedding to a man I thought was my soul mate. Amber, my best friend in the whole world, was right by my side the entire time. Everything was going well until about five months ago when I found out they were sleeping together."

Theo's jaw drops open. "What? Are you serious?"

"I sure am. The two most important people in my life betrayed me."

Each time I tell the story, it feels like I'm reliving it all over again. The moment I saw them together is so vivid in my mind, like it just happened. It still cuts as deep as it did that day.

"How long was it going on?"

"Over a year," I say. "I'm still not sure how I was so oblivious, but they went out of their way to cover their tracks. Those two could cover up a murder, and no one would have a clue."

He shakes his head. "I don't know what to say. That's awful."

"Anyway, now you can see why my life was literally crumbling around me," I tell him. "My whole world was intertwined with Dustin and Amber. We had the same social circle, went to the same places, and to complicate things more, our families are really tight. I couldn't go anywhere without the constant reminder of how they broke my heart."

He shakes his head. "I don't understand how they could do that to you—and continue on like everything was normal."

I shrug.

Theo places a perfect omelet in front of me, complete with a side of fresh berries.

"Here you go. This is your official 'Welcome to Miami' breakfast."

I smile. "Wow. This looks delicious. Is there anything you can't do?"

"Hmm … I'll get back to you on that," he says playfully.

I don't waste any time taking a bite. As soon as the eggs hit my tongue, an explosion of flavors fills my mouth, and I close my eyes to savor it.

When I open my eyes, Theo is looking at me. "How is it?"

"Heavenly."

While we eat, he continues to ask me questions about Dustin and Amber. It's becoming easier to talk about it with him. For a long time, I kept it to myself because I didn't want to face the embarrassment or make anyone choose sides.

"Amber and I have been friends since middle school. We'd been through so much together, I honestly never suspected she would do something so terrible to me," I say in between bites.

"Are they still together?"

I nod. "Yes. As far as I know. Although I wonder how long it will take them to drive each other crazy. They're actually a lot alike, both high energy and intense. I'm more easygoing— or at least I used to be. Unfortunately, this situation has made me more uptight." I pause as I collect my thoughts. "It's also been hard on my parents. Obviously, this caused a rift between them and Amber's parents. Naturally, they sided with her, and my parents backed me. Dustin and Amber's actions have had lasting effects on so many people, but I guess that didn't matter to them."

The worst part for me was having to walk away from everything. Yes, I could've stayed and picked up the pieces of my shattered heart, but everywhere I turned was a reminder of their lies.

"So, that brings me to now," I continue. "My sister-in-law's sister owns a real estate company down here. Not only was it a great opportunity, but living in Miami made it an even sweeter deal, and it was too good to pass up."

He points his fork at me. "Well, if it's any consolation, I'm glad you're here."

I feel a jolt shoot through my body. I can't deny there's some attraction between Theo and me. At the same time, allowing myself to get involved with anyone right now is not a good idea. My focus should be on work, not to mention I'm still healing from my broken heart.

"I appreciate that," I say softly. "I didn't have much support when I made this decision. I know a lot of people think I'm foolish for walking away from my job, and my mother thinks Miami is the most dangerous place in the world. I can't tell you how many times she's expressed her concern for my safety. She even bought me a Taser and a box of pepper spray."

He cringes. "Damn. I'm glad you didn't have them with you yesterday."

I laugh. "Oh, my mother would've lost her mind if she knew there was a strange man lurking around my backyard."

He folds his arms and rests them on the counter. "So, what would she think about you being here this morning?"

Something stirs inside me.

"She'd be furious. It was bad enough I go into a car with you. Now I'm in your house without my phone, and no one knows where I am."

He raises his eyebrows. "Are you nervous?"

I shake my head and clasp my hands together. "Not at all. I feel very comfortable with you."

He moves closer to me, his grey eyes staring into mine. "Good."

A strange feeling sweeps through my body, and suddenly I wonder what it'd be like to feel his lips on mine. *What's happening to me?*

"Since you made breakfast, I'll clean up," I say, quickly hopping off the barstool.

I pick up our plates and walk to the sink. Theo follows my lead and begins putting the food back into the fridge while I rinse the dishes. Neither of us says anything for a few minutes, and Theo joins me at the sink.

"Gabby, I really admire you."

I scoff. "Why?"

He folds his arms to his chest and leans against the counter. "Your life was turned upside down, and you took a huge leap starting over. Most people wouldn't have that kind of courage."

"Hah, I don't know if I'd call it courage or running away from my problems. Either way, I'm committed to making the most of my new life."

"Well, if you need anything, I'm here," he says softly.

Part of me wonders if Theo is too good to be true. He's attractive, polite, sexy and makes a fantastic omelet.

Granted, Lila doesn't think much of him, but she's most definitely jaded based on their past.

"That means a lot. It's hard to move to a new place and not know a soul. I've been surrounded by friends and family my entire life."

I reach for a towel to dry my hands, and my face is now inches from Theo's. My heart begins to race as that same feeling I had in Theo's car takes over me. Before I know what's happening, Theo places his hand on my cheek and moves his mouth closer to mine. I don't waste any time wrapping my arms around his neck and letting him kiss me. His soft lips are moving slowly against mine, and his hands are on my waist.

This is going against every promise I made to myself, but I don't care.

Theo is the first to stop and pull back. "I'm sorry."

I frown. "That's something every woman wants to hear after being kissed."

"Oh, no! I'm not sorry about the kiss. I just don't want you to think I'm trying to take advantage of the new girl in town."

"You mean you weren't trying to seduce me with your mad cooking skills and delicious breakfast?" I tease.

"Darn it, you figured me out," he says, pushing my hair behind my shoulder. "What about you? Were you trying to seduce me with your fuzzy slippers and wild morning hair?"

We both start laughing.

"Yes, because I look so sexy right now."

He steps back and looks me up and down. "Actually, you do."

He takes my face in his hands once again and gives me one more kiss.

"I really should get going," I tell him. "It's my first day at my new job, and my roommates might be wondering where I am."

He nods. "Yeah, Lila isn't going to be happy when she finds out you were over here making out with me."

The mention of Lila reminds me about her and Cal.

"By the way, Lila told me she dated Dr. Sims."

"A long time ago," Theo says. "She blamed me for their break-up."

That's exactly the way Lila described it, but like my mother says, there are always three sides to every story.

"That's basically what she told me too." Although she was a bit more dramatic when she said that Theo destroyed her life.

"It's not my fault Cal broke up with her," he insists. "Lila told him that her ex-boyfriend was coming back to town and she needed to talk to him. She was totally making out with the guy in front of her house, so of course I told my friend what I saw. Cal was disappointed after things ended, but she couldn't make up her mind between the two guys, and he wasn't going to wait around while she flip-flopped back and forth."

"Lila says that she's never felt the same about any man since."

He rolls his eyes.

I don't say anything because I don't know Lila very well either. Maybe her version of the story has changed over the years?

"Anyway, I really need to get home. Should I—?" I point to the back door.

"Oh yes, I'll walk you out."

Theo leads me to the gate that separates our houses.

"Thanks again for breakfast."

He smiles. "Anytime. And please let me know if you need anything else. I'm right here."

We both stand awkwardly, and once again I'm having a difficult time leaving.

"Bye, Theo."

I start walk away when I feel his hand on my arm.

When I turn around, he kisses me again. This time his kiss is more urgent, and I don't fight it.

This type of behavior is completely out of character for me. I thought I'd found my forever with Dustin, and he destroyed that. Maybe embracing my new life and being a little carefree will do me some good.

"Good luck today," Theo whispers before walking back to his house. I don't move for a few seconds.

Oh, Miami, I think I adore you.

Chapter Five

*W*hy does it feel like I'm doing the walk of shame when I sneak back to my house? It's not like I spent the night with Theo. Yes, our morning together started before the sun came up, but that's not the same, right?

As soon as I walk into the kitchen, Reagan is sitting at the counter, eating a bowl of Lucky Charms. She's wearing black skinny jeans and a flowy peasant top. Her blonde hair is full of loose beachy waves.

She looks down at my PJs and gives me a confused look.

"Good morning. Where were you?"

I bite my lip. Why am I so nervous? I'm a grown woman. If I want to have breakfast with the hot neighbor, that's my business. At the same time there's no reason to not tell her the truth, so I launch into my explanation about not being able to sleep and how I ended up at Theo's house.

Reagan is listening intently. We've known each other for less than twenty-four hours, but she's one of those people who makes you feel like you've known them forever.

"You totally have a thing for this Theo guy, don't you?"

I put my hands on the sides of my head. "I have no idea what I'm doing," I whine. "He just seems like a genuine nice guy, and I could use all the friends I can get right now."

I leave out the part about being really attracted to him and our kiss. She doesn't have to know everything.

Reagan nods her head. "I say go for it. After the hell you've been through, you deserve some fun."

I rub my forehead. The truth is I'm not intentionally seeking Theo out. Both times I've seen him have been purely coincidence—I certainly didn't plan on him seeing me in my PJs and bedhead this morning.

"I need to get ready. Thanks for listening."

"That's what roommates are for," she calls.

I hurry to my bathroom and jump into the shower. My mind is spinning as I replay the events of my morning. *Why do my and Theo's paths continue to cross?* Despite my intense attraction to him, I meant what I said to Reagan about needing friends. Most of my relationships were strained after Dustin and I broke up. Many people I thought were my friends showed their true colors, and I felt like I was an outsider, despite being the victim of what Dustin and Amber did to me.

As I continue to get ready for my day, I think about that kiss. The old Gabby wouldn't have done that. When Dustin and I first got together, we had a slow start—we were friends first, and it was several weeks before anything like that happened.

My clothes are still in disorganized piles around the room, but I finally choose a black maxi dress under a distressed denim jacket. I carefully wrap the bandage around my wrist and quickly blow dry my hair. I can't even look at my hand without thinking about Theo.

Now I just have to break the news to Lila. I know she wasn't happy when she suspected I might be attracted to Theo, and she's more than eager to introduce me to other people.

I take one more glance at my disaster of a room. I still haven't unpacked, and ironically, I've spent more time with Theo than I have in my new home.

When I return to the kitchen, Reagan and Lila are chatting. Lila is wearing a light pink mini dress with nude wedges. Her black hair is perfectly straight.

"Good morning. How did you sleep?" she asks.

Reagan gives me a wistful look. I'm assuming she didn't say anything about my breakfast with Theo, and I appreciate that.

"I had a rough night, but that's normal for me when I'm in a new place."

"I'm heading out," Reagan says. "I was wondering if you two wanted to meet up for dinner tonight."

"I'd love it," I say.

"Sure," Lila adds.

"My friend just opened a restaurant. It's called Golden, and the reviews are great so far. I'll text you the info."

Reagan picks up her water bottle and laptop and heads out the door. I'm excited for dinner and more opportunity to get to know my new roommates better.

"I was going to suggest we ride to the office together, but I'll be with clients most of the afternoon," Lila says. "I could go back and pick you up though."

The idea of not having to parallel park does appeal, but so does food. I have to get some groceries, or I'll definitely be eating Lucky Charms for breakfast tomorrow.

"Don't worry about it, I have to go shopping this afternoon anyway." I pause as I prepare to break the Theo news to her. "Guess what happened earlier this morning?"

Lila gives me a worried look. I know I don't owe her an explanation, but I feel it's the right thing to do.

I launch into my story about my impromptu run-in and breakfast with Theo, purposely leaving out the more intimate details.

"I warned you about him," Lila reminds me. "I promise you there are dozens of decent, eligible men in this city."

She makes it sound as if I've committed myself to him and closed myself off to meeting anyone else. That's definitely not the case.

I hold up my hands in protest.

"It was only breakfast," I assure her. "We were talking outside, and I think he offered because he feels guilty about this." I point to my wrist.

"He should feel guilty," she snaps. "If he minded his own business and let you relax peacefully in the hammock, then it wouldn't have happened."

I sigh. I know it's pointless for me to try to change her opinion of him. Clearly there's years of built-up animosity that isn't going away anytime soon.

"The point is I'm not in a place to get involved with anyone right now," I say. "I'm basically starting from scratch—a man is the last thing I need."

Lila gives me a sympathetic look. "I understand. But you should always keep your options open. Good things can happen when you least expect them to, and it won't hurt to put yourself out there."

She's right, and I'm certainly not giving up on love forever.

"That's true."

I imagine Lila's brain is working overtime to steer me away from Theo. Her feelings for Cal must've been very strong for her to still hold so much disdain for Theo.

Thankfully the subject changes to Reagan's friend's restaurant when we walk out front.

I'm not the least bit surprised when I look out across the lawn to see Theo about to get into his fancy car. Admittedly, my stomach does a flip, and the memory of his arms around me flashes through my mind.

"Good morning, ladies," he calls cheerfully.

Lila scowls. "Theo, quit trying to make a move on my new roommate."

"Ah, it's great to see you too, Lila," he teases. "It's been too long."

"Not long enough," she says under her breath.

"I'll see you at the office," she says.

"Have a great day, Lila," Theo calls.

I try to hide my smile. He's definitely trying to get under her skin.

She dramatically slides her huge sunglasses onto her face and slams her car door.

Theo walks over after she pulls out of the driveway. He's changed into a pair of black slacks and a gray button-up shirt. He looks very nice, but I don't think anything could compare to seeing him exit the pool earlier this morning. That image will probably be burned into my memory for years to come.

"She certainly hasn't changed a bit, still a breath of fresh air," he says sarcastically. "Have fun living with her."

I chew on my lip. Should I be worried that my roommate and my new *friend* despise each other?

"Maybe you two need to sit down and hash things out," I suggest. "You could call a truce."

His jaw tightens. "Hmm … a truce. I'll think about that. Although I'm not the one you need to convince."

"But you'd consider it?"

He shrugs. "It depends."

"On what?"

"What's in it for me?" he asks, the corner of his mouth curling up.

Um … so many thoughts swirl through my mind.

"Just kidding. I'm willing to coexist with Lila … for you."

My heart rate begins to speed up. It would certainly make it easier on me if Theo and Lila moved on from the past.

"I'll talk to her about it," I say. "Thanks again for breakfast."

"You're welcome anytime," he says, flashing me his gorgeous smile, which causes my heart to flutter.

I slide into my car.

"Don't forget to be careful with your wrist," he calls.

"I told you I would," I say. "I always keep my promises."

Gah! It's been so long since I playfully flirted, I don't even know if I'm doing it right.

"I'll remember that," he says as he turns and strides back to his house.

As much as I wish I could stay and continue our banter, I need to get to the office. Especially because I'm probably going to have to park in the garage and walk miles uphill to get to work now. That's an exaggeration—but I would do it to avoid parallel parking.

As I make my way out of my new neighborhood and past the guard, I'm in a daze. This is definitely not how I expected to kick off life in Miami. Sprained wrist aside, I'm enjoying it.

When I finally make it to Fun in the Sun Realty after a hike from the parking garage, I'm instantly fired up. Elizabeth has created a powerhouse team and I feel so honored to be part of it.

There are two other agents besides Lila and me.

Suzanna, who's loud and intense. I usually don't get intimidated by people, but I can tell that she's a force to be reckoned with. I have no doubt she's savage when it comes to selling. Her platinum blonde hair cups her chin, and her long red fingernails match her blouse. She's wearing a power suit complete with the epic shoulder pads. She's gives me a wave as she spins slowly in her chair. I overhear her say something about negotiating closing costs.

The other agent is Javier, and the second I meet him, I know we're going to be friends.

"What do you think of Miami?" he asks. He sits down in a chair across from my desk.

"I like it a lot so far." Of course, there are several reasons for that, none of which I disclose.

"Do you know how to salsa?"

I giggle. "No. I'm not sure my body can move in those ways, and even if it could, no one wants to see that."

He waves his hand. "My sister teaches classes—she's the best in this city."

"She is," Lila chimes in from the copy machine. "I've taken a few lessons with her. You really should try it."

"Yes. It's part of the initiation of living here," Javier adds.

"Initiation?"

He laughs. "Nah. I'm kidding. But she's always looking for new business."

I understand that now more than ever, and it wouldn't hurt to put myself out there and meet more people.

"Maybe I'll give it a shot," I agree.

I try to picture myself learning how to salsa. I'm a huge fan of those dancing shows, and if I ever had the opportunity to be a contestant, I'd jump on it. Still, I'm not convinced I could keep up with the counts and not make a complete ass of myself in the process.

"We should get a group together and go," Lila exclaims. "I'm sure Reagan would be in."

Lila and Javier immediately start planning a class, and he proceeds to text his sister. I just barely turned on my laptop while trying to organize my desk. It's my first day at the agency, and they're more concerned about me learning salsa. Don't get me wrong, I appreciate them including me in their social circle, but I still have to pay my bills.

I begin making a list of what I need to hit the ground running. Networking will be huge for me. Speaking of which, Theo did tell me that he'd help to spread the word, and I'll take all the help I can get.

Elizabeth and I meet to talk about strategies to help me get going. She's been so welcoming and helpful I almost want to cry.

"I really appreciate everything you've done for me," I say after she gives me a list of potential leads. "This agency is stacked with talent—you probably didn't even need me."

She smiles. "We have an awesome team, but there's always room for one more."

Don't cry, Gabby.

"You have a very impressive resume," she adds. "I hope you don't think I only hired you because Nikki asked me to."

I twist my mouth to the side. "It crossed my mind, honestly."

My phone buzzes from on the chair next to me. When I glance at it, I see a text from a number I don't recognize.

Hello, my name is Danielle Sims. I was given your information by Theo Jorgenson. I'm interested in listing my condo for sale.

Am I dreaming? Theo steps up once again, making me wonder if he's legit. Either he's really genuine, or he's a master player who's really good at the game. My head is telling me to throw my guard up, but for some crazy reason I'm not worried. I reread Danielle's text. Wait—*Sims?*

She has to be related to Cal.

"Believe it or not, it looks like I may have a potential client already," I say, holding up my phone.

Elizabeth nods knowingly. "I had no doubt you would."

I excuse myself from Elizabeth's office to reach out to this Danielle person.

She answers on the first ring and tells me she and her husband are thinking about selling their beach front condo because it's too small.

Wow. *Must be nice.*

I get some information about the condo, and we agree to meet there in a few days. Before we hang up, I nonchalantly ask her about Theo.

"Theo and my brother-in-law are friends," she tells me. "He mentioned that you were new to the area and were trying to build your client base."

I knew it.

"What's your brother-in-law's name?

"Cal. Do you know him?"

I glance over at Lila who's also on the phone. *What are the chances?*

For such a big city, it's certainly feels like a small world around here.

"I met him yesterday. I hurt my wrist and Theo took me to his office."

"Oh, that's so funny," she says. "Anyway, my husband told me to reach out to you this morning."

When I finish my conversation with Danielle, I'm feeling really good. It takes all of my willpower to keep from jumping on my desk and dancing around. It's only been a few hours, and I already have a huge prospect—thanks to Theo. I didn't think my day could get better than breakfast with him, but obviously I was wrong.

Chapter Six

"I'd like to make a toast," Reagan says, holding up her Diet Coke. Apparently, she only drinks alcohol once a week, and last night was it.

I'm not much of a drinker either, but I have a lot to celebrate today, so I join Lila in a little indulgence. She and I follow Reagan's lead and hold up our wine glasses.

"To new friends and new adventures," Reagan cheers.

My mind flips to the image of Theo making me breakfast. Yes, I'll definitely drink to new adventures.

I have no complaints about my first day at Fun in the Sun Realty. I had a feeling I was going to like working there from the second I walked through those doors, and I was right. The energy is infectious, and my co-workers are great.

Javier is hysterical, and I can't believe I'm saying this, but I'm actually looking forward to taking a salsa class with him. Suzanna is a little standoffish, but Lila assured me that she takes a while to warm up to people, which is totally fine with me.

After her toast, Reagan starts making suggestions as we study the menu.

"Dante used to make us the lemon parmesan chicken. It's mouthwatering."

Lila looks at her phone and groans.

"I need some advice," she whines. I have a feeling she's not referring to the menu options. "Somehow I ended up with two dates to the same charity event. I have to cancel on one of them, and I feel terrible about it."

I give her a confused look. "How did that happen?"

She purses her lips. "Well—I couldn't decide between Enrique and Jordan. So, I said yes to both, and now I'm in a bind."

Poor Enrique. I don't even know the guy, and I feel sorry for him. I remember Lila was talking to him when she showed up at the agency yesterday. I thought she was trying to let him down gently, and now she might cancel on him? Ah … I forgot how tangled dating life can be.

"Well, who would you rather go with?" Reagan asks.

Lila shrugs. "Probably Jordan. Enrique is cute and sweet, but Jordan is so yummy. And we have amazing chemistry."

"Poor you," I tease. "Choosing between two sweet and yummy men must be very difficult."

Lila lets out a dramatic sigh. "It's torture."

"I think you should give the sweet one a chance," Reagan chimes in.

The server interrupts our conversation to pour water into our glasses and take our order. I finally choose the maple-glazed salmon, based on the server's recommendations.

"This place is really nice," Lila says. "That chandelier is exquisite."

I have to admit Golden is very impressive. From the outside it's just a plain brick building, but inside is gorgeous. There are touches of gold everywhere, the vaulted ceilings really open up the space, and there's a grand golden chandelier hanging in the middle of the dining room.

"Thanks for making the suggestion. I can't wait to try the food."

"Dante is an amazing chef," Reagan gushes. "He'd cook for a group of us on the weekends when we were in college. We all told him he should drop out and go to culinary school." She pauses. "And here we are. I'm so proud of him."

Lila and I glance at each other. I don't know who this Dante guy is, but it's obvious that Reagan is very fond of him.

"Okay … so tell us about Dante?" Lila asks. "Is he hot? Dante —that name rolls off the tongue just right."

I giggle, and Reagan turns bright red. I guess that's her answer to Lila's question.

"He's a good-looking guy. We've known each other a long time. It's funny that we both ended up in Miami. Of course, he's been here a lot longer than me. I'm not sure I would've come here if it weren't for my sister."

I keep forgetting that Reagan is from Illinois. In fact, I still don't know much about her. She seems really easygoing and low maintenance, which is great because Lila is definitely more intense. Unfortunately, my drama monopolized most of our conversation last night. And to top things off, I roll into the house in my PJs after having an impromptu breakfast with Theo. I have to wonder if my new roommates think I'm a hot mess.

That would be an accurate description of my life over the past several months. In my defense, the two people I trusted more than anyone devastated me.

"Is Dante here tonight?" Lila asks.

Reagan gets a panicked look. "I'm sure he is, but I don't want to bother him."

"Maybe we could see him for a minute—you know, to thank him for the wonderful meal," I suggest.

Granted, we haven't eaten yet, and the food could be complete crap. I don't say that out loud though.

"Right on time," Lila exclaims, practically jumping out of her chair.

She throws her arms around a man with brown spiked hair and glasses then does the same to another guy, who reminds me of Joey from *Friends*.

She waves to our server and asks if he can bring over two more chairs.

I glance at Reagan who raises her eyebrows. It doesn't take me long to figure out that these are two of the men Lila wanted to introduce us to.

"Harry and Paul, these are my new roommates," she says excitedly.

We all introduce ourselves and make the usual small talk—where we are from, what we do for work, and then come the questions about what happened to my wrist.

The fact that I fell out of hammock seems to amuse everyone. The guys are both friendly and nice looking, but in the back of my mind I know this is Lila' attempt to steer me away from Theo. I don't mind meeting them though because I'm open to all possibilities. It would be ridiculous to close myself off after a handful of moments with Theo.

I'm not going to lie though—I'd love to accidentally catch him swimming laps again. When I made the decision to come to Miami, I was hopeful it would be an easy transition, and I have no complaints so far. That doesn't mean I'm naïve enough to think that it's going to be smooth sailing the whole way.

"I worked in Orlando for a few years," Harry tells me. "I liked it, but Miami is more my speed. I think you'll love it here."

"I already do," I say with a grin.

Like clockwork, my phone buzzes from beside me. There's a tiny part of me that's hoping it's another referral from Theo.

When I pick it up, I see a text from Nikki.

Call me when you get a chance.

For some reason a feeling of dread washes over me. My sister-in-law is one of those people who doesn't like talking on the phone. She'd rather text an entire novel, so her request strikes me as odd.

"Are you okay?" Reagan asks under her breath.

"Yeah, why?"

"You got a strange look on your face."

I hold up my phone. "It's just a text from home. I'm sure it's not a big deal."

That's a total lie. I consider excusing myself to call Nikki back, but I don't want to be rude. She'd let me know if it were an emergency.

"Gabby and I are taking a salsa class," Lila announces. "You guys need to join us."

Joey—I mean, Paul—adamantly shakes his head. "Not happening. No one wants to see me shaking anything, and I have no rhythm, so the whole thing would be a nightmare."

Harry takes a sip of his beer. "I'll do it. It wouldn't be the first time I embarrassed myself in front of a bunch of people."

Our server returns with a tray of food. Harry and Paul place their orders, and we continue talking about all the must do's in the area.

"My uncle has a house down in Islamorada," Harry tells us. "I can use it anytime I want. We could get a group together and head down there anytime."

"It's gorgeous," Lila chimes in. "And I should know because I sold it to him."

"How long have you known each other?" I ask.

Harry and Lila look at each other.

"Three years, right?" Lila says.

"Yep, we broke up six months after we met," Harry says. "And we've been friends ever since."

Wait, what? Harry and Lila dated? I really hope Lila isn't trying to set me up with her ex. There are so many things wrong with that.

"You two were together?" Reagan asks.

I love how she comes out and asks exactly what I'm thinking.

"Yes," Harry says fondly. "Until we realized we weren't compatible at all. It takes a stronger man than me to put up with her."

Lila nods. "At least you admit it."

"He cried for about a day," Paul announces.

"Most men have a hard time getting over me," Lila says. "Except Cal Sims."

There she goes again. She gets a faraway look in her eyes every time she mentions him. I really should ask Theo about it, or maybe skip him and bring it up to Dr. Sims himself.

"This salmon is fantastic," I exclaim in between bites. I finish every morsel and refrain from licking the plate, even though I'm tempted.

"Reagan, I think we should offer our compliments to the chef."

She gets a nervous look on her face. "Okay, as long as he's not busy. I don't want to interrupt him."

Doesn't the chef like to chat with the customers? I've seen it on Gordon Ramsay's show a bunch of times. Although on his show, all hell is usually breaking loose.

When the waiter returns, I ask him if Chef Dante is available to come out for a minute.

"Definitely. He loves getting feedback. I'll tell him you'd like to speak with him."

Reagan nonchalantly wipes the corners of her mouth and runs her fingers through her hair.

Oh yes, she most definitely has a crush on the chef.

Barely a minute goes by when I see a tall man in a white chef's coat walking toward our table. He has dark brown hair, and I know right away that it's Dante. Of course, when Reagan's face lights up like a Christmas tree, that confirms it.

"Good evening, ladies and gentlemen." He stands behind Reagan and gives her shoulders a squeeze. You can almost see her body melt at his touch. "How is everything tasting?"

"That was the best salmon I've ever had," I say.

I'm being completely honest—I don't remember the last time I tasted something so good.

"Fantastic," Lila chimes in. "And we aren't just saying that because you're Reagan's friend."

"I'm glad to hear that," he says with a laugh.

Dante offers us a round of drinks and dessert on the house, which makes us like him even more. Who wouldn't love free booze and sugar?

When he kneels down to eye level with Reagan, I worry she might pass out from pure joy. I watch her expression as he whispers something to her. She's absolutely giddy, and that confirms my suspicions that she thinks of him as more than a friend.

"Thanks for coming in tonight," Dante says. "I hope you'll all return, and please tell your friends about us."

Reagan can't stop smiling after he leaves. Lila gives me a look, and I know she's thinking the same thing I am.

"I think we should come here at least once a week," I suggest. "I'm sure it will be good for business and help Dante build his regular clientele."

"I'm totally down for that," Lila agrees.

Reagan looks like she might burst into tears.

The subject shifts from dreamy chef Dante. Harry starts asking me more questions about Orlando, while Paul chats with Lila and Reagan.

Admittedly, I'm stuck on the fact that he and Lila were in a relationship. I refuse to get involved with men my friends have dated. It's a bit of a trigger for me, with good reason.

When I finally get home from Golden, I try calling Nikki, but her phone goes straight to voice mail. Today was such a great day, but an uneasy feeling is still gnawing at me. My intuition has become spot-on, which usually means something is about to happen. I hate the fact that I'm so jaded because I never used to be this way. Thankfully, I managed to squeeze in a quick trip to the grocery store, so I won't have to depend on Theo to feed me or survive on cereal alone. And if the sky falls in, I have an adequate amount of comfort food at my fingertips.

As soon as I finish changing into my pajamas, which tonight is a large T-shirt and old shorts, my phone rings.

When I see Nikki's number, my stomach lurches.

"Hello."

"Hey, how was your first day?" she asks cheerfully.

"It was—really good, actually." Maybe I overreacted to her text. It wouldn't be the first time.

"Is everything okay there?" I ask.

She doesn't say anything for a few seconds, which confirms my uneasy feeling.

"Yes …"

"That doesn't sound very convincing. What's going on?"

"Everything is okay—I just have some news."

I sit down on the edge of my bed and brace myself because I already know I'm not going to like what I'm about to hear.

Chapter Seven

*A*fter five months I thought I'd come to terms with my engagement ending. I knew Dustin and Amber continued their relationship, but I really believed that their fling would run its course and they'd both end up miserable and alone. It takes a few minutes to process the news that they're now engaged and basically continuing with the wedding plans Amber so graciously helped me with.

How lame is it to have the same wedding as your former best friend? Couldn't she come up with ideas on her own instead of basically stealing my wedding right along with my fiancé?

Granted Amber and I have a lot of similar interests and taste, so it's not completely farfetched that she'd want the same color scheme, venue, flowers, and entertainment. We were inseparable for most of our lives, so it's no surprise that we're alike in many ways. Obviously, Dustin thought so too.

"Are you okay?" Nikki asks after a few minutes. "As soon as I heard, I wanted to be the one to tell you. I thought it might be easier coming from me. Jason even told your parents to let me break the news."

My brother is much better at handling our parents than I am, especially our mother. I know this has been hard on them too, losing their best friends after so many years is not easy. I'm still not sure if my mother was more upset about my engagement ending or losing Amber's parents. And I was never fully convinced she liked Dustin. She said she did, but their interaction always seemed awkward.

"Thank you for telling me," I say. "I don't know what to feel anymore. The one thing I'm sure about is that I'm so glad I'm here right now. I think the news would be harder to face if I were still in Orlando."

"Oh, absolutely," she insists. "Let's talk about that. How's the agency? Is Lizzy being nice to you? She can be super bossy and moody—well, as a sister. I'm not sure how she'd be as a boss, probably the same."

I smile to myself.

"Elizabeth is great, and so is everyone else I work with for the most part," I tell her. "My roommates are really fun—we went out to dinner tonight, and I've already met some other people."

"That's great news," she says, sounding relieved. "It was the right decision for you."

I almost tell her about Theo, but for some reason I stop myself. I probably need to press the pause button on that anyway. It's much too soon to get involved with anyone, and the last thing I need is a rebound fling.

"Thank you for standing by me through everything," I say, feeling tears threaten my eyes. "I don't know what I'd do without you."

"Girl, you're my sister. I got your back."

The tears that were building are now sliding down my cheeks. I tell Nikki that I'll call her back because I need a moment. I drop the phone on the bed next to me, put my face in my hands and let everything out. The emotions that have been building since the moment I left Orlando are finally coming to the surface.

I'm not even upset about Dustin and Amber's engagement—well, maybe I am a little. But I'm the one who had to leave everything behind because it was too painful. They are continuing to live their lives without having to make any changes. I can only hope that karma truly does exist and that it's coming for them.

When I finally pull myself together after my meltdown, I take a few breaths and wash my face. My eyes are still red and puffy, but at least I no longer have mascara running down my cheeks. I tiptoe to the kitchen to get some water. Neither of my roommates are around, so I sink down into Lila's cozy white couch with my glass. I lean my head back and stare at the ceiling.

For several nights after walking in on Dustin with Amber, I couldn't sleep. I'd lay in my bed and toss and turn for hours trying to figure out what went wrong and kicking myself for not realizing what was happening behind my back. Confronting them was the icing on the cake. Dustin repeatedly apologized for hurting me, and Amber bawled her eyes out and told me how much I meant to her. The turning point was the moment I asked them if they were willing to end their relationship, and everything went radio silent. I knew right away that they made their choice—and it wasn't me.

When I stretch my arms over my head, the bandage on my wrist catches my eye. I drag myself off the couch and make my way outside. It's a typical night in Florida, the air is thick and sticky with at least eighty-five percent humidity.

I stand next to the illuminated pool and dip my toe in. The sound of the water falling over the rocks is soothing and peaceful. Maybe I should take a page out of Theo's book and swim a few laps. Some physical activity might be exactly what I need.

The sting of the engagement news isn't going away anytime soon, so I need to do something to take my mind off it.

Before I have a chance to gather my thoughts, I start walking toward Theo's house. It's after eleven o'clock, so he could be fast asleep, especially since he'll probably be awake before the sun rises again. That doesn't stop me from making my way through the gate and into his backyard. I have no idea what I'm doing here, but it seems like my best option.

There aren't any lights on in the house, but I knock loudly on the glass door anyway. All of a sudden, I feel ridiculous—this poor guy doesn't need me interrupting his evening.

I turn to walk away when a light comes on in the house. My heart starts beating against the walls of my chest when I see Theo. He's wearing a pair of sweatpants, and he's shirtless once again. Obviously, the man doesn't like wearing anything on his upper torso. He's also wearing a pair of square-framed glasses that add a whole other level to his hotness. Admittedly, it's a pleasant distraction from everything else going on. He waves when he seems me and opens the door.

"Hey, Gabby. What's—" He stops and stares at my face.

"What happened? Are you okay?"

The tears may have stopped falling, but my swollen eyes are all the proof he needs to know something's wrong.

"Hey. I'm sorry to bother you so late. You're probably about to go to bed."

He shakes his head. "I was just lying in bed watching baseball highlights. Come in."

I follow Theo into the house and fold my arms against my chest. I look down at my T-shirt and shorts. Maybe someday Theo will see me looking halfway decent. During most of our interactions thus far I've been facedown under a hammock and in my pajamas. Not the impression I would normally want to make, but it's too late for that.

"Can I get you something to drink?"

I shake my head. "I don't even know why I'm here," I say with a nervous laugh. "I guess I just needed to talk to someone."

Why did I come over here? I'm sure Reagan and Lila would've given me an ear to listen and shoulder to cry on if I needed it.

"Don't worry about it," he says softly. He points to the leather sectional couch, and I sit down on the edge of one of the seats.

Theo sits next to me, and my eyes drift toward his abs. There's at least six of them, possibly eight if I look closely. All of those morning laps are certainly paying off.

"You probably think I'm super high maintenance," I say.

He chuckles. "Nonsense. Why would I think that?"

I chew on my lower lip.

"I got some news from home a little while ago, and I'm trying to process." I point to my eyes. "Obviously, I'm not doing a good job of it."

He gives me a sympathetic look. It could also be pity—but whatever.

"Okay. Tell me what happened. Is your family okay?"

I rub my temples with my fingertips.

"My ex and my best friend are getting married."

"Aw man, that's rough," he says, shaking his head.

"I guess I should be flattered—she's using my wedding plans." I pause as I try to swallow the lump that's building in my throat again.

"How did you find out?"

As I tell him about Nikki's phone call, I get choked up.

"I can't believe I'm still crying about this," I wail, dabbing the corners of my eyes. "It's so stupid."

Theo leans his head to the side. "It's not."

"I don't want to give them the satisfaction, but even hundreds of miles away they're still affecting me," I exclaim. "Running away didn't change anything."

Theo slides a little closer to me, and for some reason it makes me relax a little. "Do you remember what I said to you this morning?"

I shrug. Everything before our kiss is kind of fuzzy.

"I told you that I admired you for taking a chance and starting over in a new city. You may think of it as running away from your problems, but I see it as taking a stand and showing you weren't just going to sulk because your relationship was over."

I cover my eyes in hopes that it will somehow make the tears stop.

Theo places his hand on my back but doesn't say anything. I appreciate that he's letting me express how I'm feeling. He's not trying to make me talk about it or asking lots of questions. This night has been such a whirlwind, and I'm still not sure how or why I ended up here. There's definitely something about being with Theo that makes me feel safe.

When I finally pull myself together, I thank him for letting me vent.

"I should probably go—I know you have to get up early." I start to move off the couch, but he stops me.

"Why don't you stay for a little while? We don't have to talk about anything if you don't want to. We can put on a movie or watch TV. I have popcorn."

That sounds wonderful, and before I have a chance to respond, he grabs a remote from the console and flips on his flatscreen TV.

"Holy crap, that TV is huge. What size is it?"

"Eighty-five inches," he brags.

"A Tesla and eighty-five-inch TV?" I tease. "My brother and you would be besties."

"Awesome. Yeah, I'm kind of bougie."

I giggle. "You said it, not me."

"I have expensive taste, just like my mother did," he says. "But I work hard for everything I have."

Hmm … did his mother pass away? It occurs to me that I don't know much about his family except that they've lived in this house for years. I want to ask him, but I'm so emotionally drained right now.

He continues to flip through the channels until he comes to *Friends.*

"How about *Friends*?" he asks. "It's my favorite show."

I smile. "I love it."

"Oh, it's the one where they're in Vegas," he says excitedly. He drops the remote on the couch and walks to the kitchen. I reposition my body and pull my legs under me. A few minutes later the sound and smell of popcorn begins to fill the air.

"Do you want a water or a soda?" he calls. "I also have beer and wine."

Ugh. The last thing I need is alcohol.

"Water is fine."

I lean my head back and stare at the TV. I didn't know what to expect when I came here, but this couldn't be more perfect. My roommates would probably want to discuss every little detail and I'm so done.

A few minutes later Theo returns with two water bottles and a bowl of popcorn. He opens a cabinet under the TV and pulls out a fluffy white blanket. He unfolds it and drapes it over me.

"I'll be right back. I'm just going to put a shirt on."

Bummer.

There's a part of me that wants to burst into tears again, but in a good way. I pull the blanket up to my chest. Theo is extremely considerate, and it makes me wonder how the man is still single.

When he returns, he's wearing a blue T-shirt. It fits him just right, so I have no complaints. He sits next to me, but not too close. I hand him the bowl of popcorn.

"Are you sure you don't need to go to sleep? I can leave."

He reaches into the bowl and grabs a handful of popcorn.

"Nope."

The only sounds in the room are from the crunch of popcorn and the TV, but the silence isn't uncomfortable at all. If anything, it's the most serene I've felt in months.

"Who's your favorite character on this show?" he asks finally.

I take a sip of water to clear my throat.

"Hmm—I really like Phoebe. What about you?"

"Ross."

I snort. "What? Why? No one likes Ross."

He shrugs. "Exactly. I feel bad for him."

I laugh loudly. "Well, that's very nice of you."

"I'm a nice guy."

I look down at the popcorn and the blanket. He really is.

"Despite what your roommate says about me," he adds.

I cringe. "That reminds me—I have a question."

"Okay, I have an answer."

"Is Dr. Sims married or seeing anyone?"

A mischievous smile spreads across his face. "Why? Do you think he's cute?"

I playfully hit him on his arm. "I actually didn't pay much attention. If you recall, I had pain shooting through my arm."

He nods. "Fair enough. Then why are you asking about Cal's love life?"

I'm not going to come out and tell him that I want to play matchmaker, but that's exactly what I was thinking.

"Well—from what Lila has told me, the main reason she dislikes you so much is because of Cal."

He presses his lips together. "So, you're asking for Lila?"

"Yes."

"Sorry to disappoint you, but Cal has a serious girlfriend," he says. "I'm not sure why he hasn't proposed yet. She's great."

All my hopes are dashed by this news. I thought if I could help Lila and Cal reconnect, then that would soften her heart toward Theo.

Talking about Cal reminds me of my meeting with Danielle. I haven't even told Theo about it yet.

"Oh, my goodness, I'm the worst," I announce. "With everything that happened tonight, I completely forgot to thank you for referring me to Danielle Sims."

He waves his hand. "It's nothing."

"Are you kidding?" I exclaim. "You've been amazing since I met you. You take me to urgent care, make me breakfast, and refer me a potential client. Never mind that I just knocked on your door to cry on your shoulder."

"Well, when you put it like that—I *am* pretty awesome."

I laugh out loud. Theo has such a good personality. It's hard to stay upset when he's around.

"Your laugh is cute," he says.

My face grows hot, and I cover my cheeks with my hands. "Thanks. I feel like this is the first time I've really laughed in months."

"I'm happy that I could help you with that."

There are only a few popcorn kernels left, and we've moved the bowl to the floor. And somehow, we've edged closer to each other on the couch.

"Tell me more about yourself," I say. "I feel like we've been talking about me since we met."

This is the absolute truth. It's been one Gabby crisis after another since our introduction under the hammock.

"I'm pretty complex. Where should I start? My hopes and dreams?"

I smile. "Sure."

He tells me about traveling with his job in sports marketing and living in different cities. His mother passed almost two years ago, and his father recently got remarried to the nicest woman he's ever met.

"When my father married Maggie, he moved into her house," he tells me. "That's why I'm here now. After I came back from Dallas, I figured I'd live here until I decide what's next for me."

I nod. "I'm sorry about your mom."

"Yes, it was difficult, even though we weren't very close. Don't get me wrong—she was a good mother, just not very warm or nurturing." He stops and stares off into space for a moment. I'd love to learn more about Theo, but I don't want to force him to talk about a difficult subject. Just like he didn't force me to talk about Dustin and Amber.

"Anyway, I'm relieved my dad has someone now," he continues. "He told me I could stay here as long as I need to, and then we'll put it on the market."

I look around. "It's a great house. You'll have no problem selling."

He smiles. "About that, do you think you could recommend a good realtor?"

I give a thoughtful look. "I'm sure I could."

Theo yawns widely.

"Okay, it's time for me to go. You've been up since five."

He shakes his head. "I'm fine."

I stand up and begin to fold the blanket. "You've been so great. Thanks for … everything."

We both lean down to pick up the popcorn bowl, and as we rise up our faces are a few inches apart.

I'm reminded of the perfect kiss we shared in his kitchen earlier this morning, and while I'd love more than anything to repeat those few moments, it's not the right time.

"I'll walk you out," Theo says softly.

I'm not sure how he knows what I'm thinking, but once again he surprises me. He could've totally taken advantage of my state of mind, and I wouldn't have resisted. This makes me like him even more than I already do.

Chapter Eight

When I open my eyes, the sun is pouring into my room. It's seven o'clock, and I can't remember the last time I slept in this late.

Clearly the insomnia had finally caught up to me because as soon as my head hit the pillow, I was out. I exhale loudly as roll over and pull the comforter up to my chin. All the memories from last night come rushing back to me, starting with the news of Dustin and Amber's engagement and then hanging out with Theo.

Ahh … Theo.

Even though we just met, there's a part of me that feels like I've known him for longer. He's so easy to talk to and so funny. And he was so attentive last night—the way he brought me food and gave me a blanket. I can't remember the last time anyone fussed over me like that. Dustin and I had been together for so long, everything became so routine with us. Of course, now I know where his attention was.

And I know Theo was exhausted, but he still forced himself to stay awake to be there for me. He could have politely asked me to leave, but he didn't. He's a keeper for sure, and I have no doubt he'll make some woman very happy one day.

I give myself a few more minutes before I throw the comforter off me and sit on the side of the bed. I can't change what's happened in the past, but I can make the best of what's to come. It's another new day, and I'm ready for it. Tomorrow I have my meeting with Danielle Sims, and fingers crossed—we get her condo up on the market.

When I go into the kitchen, Lila is drinking a smoothie. She's wearing a matching sports bra and yoga pants.

"Good morning," she says. "I'm a terrible roommate."

I snort. "Are you kidding? Why would you say that?"

"I totally forgot to invite you to join Reagan and me at Pilates," she says. "I was in the middle of a side plank when it hit me."

As soon as she says the words "side" and "plank" together, it's enough to make me cringe. That's a big fat no for me. Give me a treadmill or a stationary bike any day, but twisting my body into intricate positions isn't for me.

"Hmm … I appreciate you thinking of me, but Pilates isn't my thing."

Lila shakes her head. "It's easier than you think."

"I'm sure it is, but I can think of a million other things I'd rather do."

Lila gives me a funny look. "Are you okay?"

I know my eyes are still puffy from the night before, but I really don't want to get into it.

"I'm fine," I say, opening a cabinet and grabbing a coffee mug.

"At least you didn't have breakfast with Theo today."

"Nope. No breakfast."

But I did go knocking on his door in tears late last night.

"It sounds like you're getting things going at work," she says. "Elizabeth said you already have a great lead."

I lean against the counter while my coffee brews.

"Yes, my potential client is Danielle Sims."

She looks confused. "Should I know who that is?"

I don't know if she's ever met Cal's brother, but I'm all about keeping lines of communication open.

"She's married to Cal's brother."

Lila's eyes grow wide. "Oh, I know Kevin, but I never met his wife."

"Theo actually referred her to me," I add.

She frowns. "He's really laying it on thick, isn't he? But I'd say go for it."

Wait. I'm confused. *Is she telling me to go for Theo?*

"You should take full advantage of all the contacts he has." She lets out a wicked laugh as she heads to her room.

I certainly don't intend to use Theo for anything, but as a friend I appreciate any help he can give me.

After staring into the fridge for a few seconds, I finally decide to make some avocado toast. It's not Theo's perfect omelet, but it's a close second.

When I return to my room to get ready, my phone rings. I groan when I see my mother's number. I'm already prepared for the questions and a lecture about staying safe in this city.

"Hey, Mom."

"Good morning. I'm glad you answered," she says. "I wasn't sure if you'd be busy."

Really? It's seven thirty in the morning. Where did she think I'd be?

"I'm about to jump into the shower to get ready for my day."

As expected she launches into questions about Lila's house and the area where I live.

"Mom, you know I moved into a gated community."

I told her this more times than I can count. I even sent her the link to the community Facebook page so she could research it.

"Well, you can never be too careful," she reminds me. "What about your roommates? Do they seem normal?"

"How would you define normal?" I tease.

"Gabrielle," she scolds. "There's a movie called *Single White Female*. I urge you to watch it."

"Mom."

"You never know who people really are until you're around them for a while," she reminds me.

That's true. It took three years to find out the type of man Dustin was.

"My roommates are really nice," I tell her. "And so are my co-workers. I've met some awesome people down here."

She sighs. "Okay. Just please don't let your guard down."

"I know, Mom."

She doesn't say anything for a few seconds. I wonder if she's going to bring up Dustin and Amber's engagement. It's definitely a sensitive subject for all of us.

"I'm really excited about the new life I'm building here."

"Mmm …"

Is she even listening to me?

"Mom, I spoke to Nikki last night."

"Oh?"

"You don't have to avoid the subject."

"Gabrielle, you know it's terribly difficult for me to talk about."

I scoff. "Yeah, I know a little something about that."

This isn't the first time we've had a conversation like this.

"I know, honey," she says. "Dustin has caused so much pain. Breaking my baby girl's heart and ruining life-long friendships. I wish he'd never come into our lives."

I fall back on the bed. "Well, Amber had a little something to do with it too. Don't excuse her behavior."

"I'm not," she snaps.

I glance at the time. "As much as I'd love to chat some more, I have to get ready for work."

It takes me another five minutes to convince her that I have my Taser and pepper spray in my car and ready to activate when and if I'm in a dangerous situation.

There's no way I'm telling her anything about Theo. What she doesn't know won't hurt her anyway.

Chapter Nine

I should've moved to Miami years ago. I'm completely in awe of Danielle Sims' condo, and if I could afford it, I'd buy it in a heartbeat. I pulled all the comps from the area before I arrived, and since the property appears to be in perfect condition, I think we can get it listed as soon as possible.

"This a beautiful place," I say.

She nods. "Yes, but we're ready for something bigger."

She points to the tiny bump on her stomach.

"Oh, wow, congratulations."

She beams. "Thank you. We've been trying for a while, so this is big news for our family."

We continue chatting about other areas, and she tells me where they're looking to purchase.

"I'm hoping you can help us with that too," she says.

"Oh, my goodness, absolutely." I nod as I hold in any tears that might try to escape my eyes. I need to keep this professional. Having an emotional breakdown isn't good for business.

"Well, we trust Theo, and he says you were one of the best agents back in Orlando."

My heart begins to pound. I'm not sure how I'll ever be able to repay Theo.

"He's been so nice since I arrived in town."

She smiles. "He's the real deal. And even after having a rough few years, he hasn't changed a bit."

I'm not sure if she's talking about Theo's mother's death or something else, and I'm not going to ask her. I certainly don't want to pry into Theo's life. Although he knows everything about mine.

"He's quite a catch too," she adds. "Kevin and I are setting him up with a friend of ours. I'm telling you, they're perfect for one another. If there's such a thing as soul mates—it's those two."

A wave of jealousy comes over me when she mentions setting Theo up with someone else. Not that I'm surprised because Theo is a catch. I've been wondering how he hasn't been snatched up yet.

"Okay, so you think we can sell this beauty?" Danielle asks, changing the subject.

"Absolutely," I say, plastering a big smile on my face.

I push all thoughts of Theo and his potential soul mate out of my mind. The only thing that matters in this moment is my job, and that's what I'm going to concentrate on.

When I return to the office, I get right to work on the listing and start researching some properties for Danielle and Kevin to look at, including one in my neighborhood.

My mind wanders a few times to what Danielle said about Theo.

I haven't spoken to him since showing up at his house after talking to Nikki. It's probably a good thing, though, because seeing him every day could easily start to become habit.

Ugh. It's so frustrating because this is exactly what I was hoping to avoid. I told myself to stay away from men, especially because I've been in such a vulnerable place. It doesn't help that Theo is charming, good-looking, and kind. All those reasons are why I should hit slow down before I get in too deep.

"How was your meeting?" Lila asks, dragging me out of my thoughts.

"It was—really good."

Lila frowns. "What happened?"

"Nothing—why."

"You look perplexed."

There's no way I'm discussing Theo with her.

"I'm just anxious to get things going," I tell her. "You know how you want to jump in and do everything all at once."

Lila takes the bait, and I breathe a sigh of relief. It's time for me to follow through on what I planned to do when I moved here. This is my chance to hit restart, and I'm not letting anything, or anyone stand in my way.

When I get home from work, I'm exhausted. My plan for the night is to finally organize my room. No more accidentally-on-purpose running into Theo or rushing over to his house in a panic.

"Hey, girl."

When I walk into the kitchen Reagan is sitting at the counter.

Hold on. *That's not Reagan.* But whoever it is looks exactly like her. This girl has the same brown eyes, but her hair is a bit darker blonde and longer.

Reagan's doppelgänger must notice the confusion on my face.

"I'm Kennedy, Reagan's sister."

I sit down on a chair and put my hand to my forehead.

"Oh, good. I thought I was finally losing it."

She laughs. "Trust me, I have that feeling at least once a day. You must be Gabby."

I nod.

"I'm extremely overprotective of my baby sister, so I forced Reagan to give me the scoop on her new roommates."

Hmm … I'm not sure how I feel about this girl knowing my life story. But I totally understand her need to protect her sister. She's probably thinking the same things as my mother, although I doubt she told Reagan to watch that movie about the roommate who goes insane.

"I'm ready," Reagan calls. She saunters into the kitchen wearing a plunging black sleeveless shirt and black skinny jeans. She looks fantastic.

"Hey, Gabby, I didn't hear you come in. I assume you met my *older* sister Kennedy."

Kennedy rolls her eyes at the older comment.

"I just did. And I like your names, by the way."

Reagan nods. "Our parents are very patriotic. Who else would name their daughters after former US presidents?"

I laugh.

"Nice shirt," Kennedy says, giving her a judgmental look.

Reagan scowls. "Don't start. I'm not interested in a lecture."

"What are you talking about?" she asks innocently.

"You obviously don't like my shirt."

"Well, it's practically falling off," Kennedy points out.

Reagan scoffs. "Are you serious? You're the queen of slutty clothes."

"Not anymore," she says with a shrug.

I stand back and watch the sisters argue about which one is the worse dresser. I have to admit I'm entertained.

"Anyway, we're going back to Golden tonight," Reagan says, finally acknowledging that I'm still in the room. "Do you want to come with us?"

Ahh … they're going to Golden. I'm sure Reagan is hoping to get a few minutes with Chef Dante. And that explains the shirt.

"Thanks for the invitation, but I have a long list of things to do tonight."

As much as I'd love to be social and have that delicious salmon again, I need to stay home.

Reagan and Kennedy leave a few minutes later, and the house is quiet. I put some pasta in a pot on the stove and head to my room to change.

I manage to dig out a pair of leggings and a white tank top from one of the various piles. Half my clothes are now hanging in the closet, and the remainder are all scattered around the room. I'm usually an organized person, so this mess is really starting to get to me.

I hear my phone ringing from somewhere. Now if only I could find it. I shift a few things on the bed and grab it just in time to answer.

"Hello."

"Gabby."

My heart sinks into my stomach, and a wave of nausea comes over me. I recognize the voice, although I don't understand why she'd be calling me.

"What do you want, Amber?"

After everything came out about the affair with Dustin, Amber tried to reach out to me a few times. It finally took my brother and Nikki to step in and tell her to stop. She claimed she wanted to explain herself, but at the same time there was no way she was letting Dustin go, and she told me that. I still think she wanted to make sure I wasn't going to fight for him.

Believe me there was no way in hell I'd take him back after what he did to me. I have way too much self-respect for that.

"Really, Gabby, you don't have to be so rude."

Typical Amber. Selfish to the core.

"You think I'm rude," I say with a laugh. "Okay, I'll humor you. Hey, Amber, it's great to hear from you. What's up?"

She doesn't say anything for a few seconds.

"Whatever. The reason I'm calling is to give you some news—"

"About your engagement?" I interrupt. "Why on earth would you need to tell me that?"

"Oh, you heard?"

This girl is so obtuse. She's conveniently forgotten that our families are friends with all the same people. There's no way she could get engaged and me not hear about it.

"Of course, I did," I snap. "I guess all those months of helping me plan gave you a nice head start on all the wedding details."

Silence.

What can she say? She knows I'm right.

"Anyway, is that all?" I ask.

"How's Miami?"

Am I really having this conversation? She calls to tell me she's engaged to my ex, and now she wants to make small talk. I should hang up on her, but my mother taught us to always finish a conversation even if we have the last word.

"My life isn't any of your concern anymore," I say firmly. "Don't call me again."

Before giving her a chance to say anything else, I end the call. With a deep inhale I sit on the edge of my bed and bury my face in my hands. Is there any escape? The reason I came to Miami was to get away from all of that drama. I can't continue to let their toxicity infringe on my new life too. As much as I want to cry, there are barely any tears left in me. Maybe this is the moment I've been waiting for? The moment to pull myself out of the ashes and be a stronger person.

I hop off the bed and start picking up things around my room. I'm more determined than ever to keep my focus and not let Amber or Dustin or my mother discourage me. I'm going to make the most of this new opportunity I've been given—and when all is said and done, I won't need to look back.

I'm in my closet folding jeans when I hear a loud beeping sound. *Is that the smoke alarm?*

Holy crap—my pasta!

I totally forgot about it thanks to stupid Amber's phone call.

As I run to the kitchen, the house is filling with smoke. I grab the pot off the stove and turn off the burner. The pasta has become a burnt mess stuck to the inside of the pot. I don't even know where the smoke alarm is, but the annoying sound continues to ring in my ears.

I open both french doors to help air out the kitchen and start waving my arms. I've only been here a few days, and now I almost burn down Lila's kitchen. I wouldn't be surprised if she kicked me out.

All of a sudden there's pounding on the front door. Maybe someone called the fire department?

Ahh ... the chaos continues.

When I fling the open the door, Theo is standing there. Once again, he shows up to rescue me in my time of need. Is this all a coincidence that he always happens to be in the right place at the right time? Not to mention, he looks as dashing as ever in his gray slacks and a white button-up shirt. His wavy black hair is pushed back with sunglasses.

"Gabby, is everything okay? I just pulled up and heard an alarm going off."

He peers behind me into the smoke-filled house.

"I was on the phone and totally forgot about my dinner," I mutter.

Seriously, what else could happen? My life has turned into a comedy since I moved to Miami, and Theo's had a front row seat.

Theo follows me inside and helps me fan the smoke away from the smoke detector. The alarm is still going off, and my head is beginning to pound.

After a few minutes the ringing finally stops, and I dramatically fall down in a chair.

"Well, that was fun," Theo says.

I shake my head. "Lila is going to wish she never let me move in."

"Nah," he says, waving his hand.

Does anything faze this man? The only time I've seen him worried was when I hurt my wrist.

"Um, hello, I could've burned down her house."

He tries to hide his smile. At least he's amused.

"She'll understand. You're not the first person to set off a smoke detector," he reminds me.

"Yeah, well now you understand why I'm such a pro at ordering takeout."

Theo looks at the pot of burnt spaghetti and makes a face.

"So, does this mean you're free for dinner?"

My stomach does a little flip, but my brain instantly steps in. I told myself I would slow down when it came to Theo.

The sound of the garage door pulls me out of my thoughts.

"What's that smell?" Lila calls.

Theo looks at me and cringes. It's too late for him to leave, so he casually leans against the counter.

"Is something burning?"

As soon as she sees Theo, she scowls. "Oh, great."

"It's totally my fault," I exclaim. "I'll buy you some new pots and pans."

"I'm not worried about that," she says, eyeing Theo.

I launch into an explanation about the phone call from Amber and forgetting the pasta.

"She actually called you?" Lila asks, sounding as shocked as I felt getting the call.

"Yep," I say. "She felt the need to call me with some news from back home."

I don't go into the details of the engagement.

"Wow. She's rotten to the core," Lila insists.

I glance at Theo, who's remained quiet.

"Anyway, Theo heard the alarm and came over to check on us."

She looks back and forth between Theo and me.

"Thanks for checking," she says, setting her bag on the counter.

"No worries," Theo replies.

Lila starts digging under the sink for air deodorizer spray. "Where's Reagan?"

I tell her about meeting Kennedy and the argument over Reagan's shirt.

"She's got it bad for Chef Dante," Lila says.

I shake my head. "You're not kidding. She definitely wanted him to notice her tonight."

Theo listens as Lila and I discuss Reagan and her crush. I should probably get him out before he overstays his welcome.

"I'll walk you out," I tell Theo.

"Sounds good. See ya, Lila."

"Bye, Theo."

As soon as we're outside, Theo lets out a sigh. "Brr ... it was chilly in there."

I giggle. "I haven't had a chance to talk to her about the truce."

"Hmm ... that might be a long shot," he says. "Anyway, how about dinner? Are you in?"

I hesitate before finally saying no. "I really want to, but I have so much to get done around here."

He nods. "I understand. Rain check?"

There are so many thoughts swirling through my head that it's almost overwhelming.

"Yeah," I say unconvincingly.

Theo looks as confused as I feel.

I can't believe I already let myself get to this point.

"I'm sorry, Theo," I say sadly. "Believe me, I'd love nothing more than to have dinner with you. I really have to get my life in order before anything …" I trail off and rub my forehead. "I just got here and …" I continue to fumble over my words as I struggle to put the brakes on whatever has been happening between us.

Theo holds up his hands to stop me. "Gabby, you don't owe me an explanation. You've been through hell and back."

Ugh. It's no surprise that he's being so understanding.

"Remember, I'm right next door if you need anything."

He gives me one last wave before turning toward his house. It takes everything in me not to run and throw my arms around him, but I know this is the way it has to be for now. Sometimes temporary sacrifices lead to the best endings.

Chapter Ten

*I*t's so wild how life takes us down different paths. A year ago, I was happily planning my dream wedding, completely oblivious to the curve ball that was coming my way.

Today I have a job in a new city, and I'm waiting with the highest amount of anticipation for a phone call about an offer on Danielle Sims' condo. We've had two showings, and one couple fell in love the second they stepped out onto the balcony overlooking the Atlantic. They made an offer an hour after their tour, and the Sims countered it. Now we wait to hear if they will take it or if the condo is still on the market.

It's been six days since I almost burned down Lila's house, and I've forced myself to stay busy ever since. I finally got unpacked and organized, signed up for a salsa class with Lila and Javier, and even stayed late at Fun in the Sun one day. Basically, I've been doing anything and everything I can to keep my mind off of Theo. I haven't seen him since I turned down his dinner invitation, and although it's been difficult,

I'm proud of myself for making the decision to slow down. Not that I haven't been tempted to pop over to his house on a few occasions. When I received the potential offer for the Sims condo, Theo was the first person I wanted to call because it wouldn't have happened without him. It took quite a bit of willpower to refrain from reaching out even just to thank him. Of course, it would've been a nice gesture, but I don't trust myself around him.

The sound of my phone buzzing pulls me out of my thoughts. It's a text from Danielle.

Any news?

I know they're also on pins and needles waiting to hear if the potential buyer takes the offer. I promised her I'd let her know ASAP but I send her a quick response anyway because that's what a good agent does.

Not yet. Sit tight.

In the meantime, I've also been in touch with a co-worker of Kevin's who's interested in selling their home. I'm definitely making the most of the connections I have so far. Hopefully, they pay off.

As the end of the day rolls around, I'm growing more nervous because I still haven't heard a word about the offer.

"Waiting is so nerve-wracking," Lila says after I check my phone for the hundredth time.

We drove to the office together today, and she's been trying to keep me distracted with casual conversation while on our way home.

"It is," I exclaim. "I know I'll feel better after I make my first sale. I'm trying to be reasonable because it hasn't been that long, but I've got bills to pay."

When we pull into our driveway, I immediately notice Theo next door putting a suitcase in his trunk. My heart begins to pound against the walls of my chest, and a wave of panic takes over. *Where is he going?*

Lila gives me a side glance but doesn't say anything before heading into the house. I wonder if she could see the worry on my face.

I wave to Theo, and a smile spreads across his face. Yes, it's only been six days, but I've really, really missed that smile.

"How are you?" he calls across the lawn.

Don't run to him, Gabby.

"I'm fine. Just staying busy in the world of real estate."

I cringe at my lame response the second the words fall out of my mouth.

We casually walk toward each other. It's probably more dignified than sprinting toward him and leaping into his arms.

"Good. I expect nothing less," he says. "I'm actually heading out of town for work."

My shoulders relax a bit when I hear that he's only going on a business trip. Seeing him with a suitcase and the thought of him not being next door makes me sick to my stomach.

Gah! Even after all my efforts, why is it so hard to get him out of my mind?

"Oh, cool. I hope you have a safe trip."

It feels like we should be saying more, but clearly we're both holding back. At least I am.

"Thank you. Are you getting settled in over there?" he asks, pointing to Lila's house.

"I am—it's finally starting to feel like home."

"And you're being careful in the kitchen," he teases.

I scowl, but a giggle manages to escape. "I haven't attempted to turn on the stove since the pasta incident."

He glances at his phone. "Whoa. I really should get going."

I nod as I try to ignore the lump that's forming in my throat.

"I'll see you soon." He hesitates for a few seconds before rushing back to his car.

"Okay. Bye, Theo."

As I wander back to my house, I feel like I've been punched in the gut. Now I'm second guessing everything. Should I have said something, maybe suggest we hang out when he returns? Man, I'm confused.

When I walk inside, Lila is sitting on the couch, scrolling through her phone.

"What's really going on with you and Theo?" she asks. "I thought you wanted to get used to life here without a man complicating it."

I nod. "Believe me, I do."

"But you really like Theo," she says knowingly.

I chew on my bottom lip. "Is it that obvious?"

She shrugs. "Probably not to most people. I just have a sense when it comes to this stuff."

I let out a frustrated sigh and fall down on the couch across from her. "It wasn't my intention, believe me. He's been so good to me since I arrived, and now I want to spend more time with him."

I finally tell her about going to Theo's after getting the news of Dustin and Amber's engagement.

"You should've come talk to me—although Reagan would probably be the better option. I'm not the most nurturing person."

I laugh. "That's the thing. I was so upset that I didn't think twice about going over there first. It felt like the natural thing to do."

She groans. "I can't believe I'm going to say this."

"Then don't."

"Are you sure?" she asks.

"No. Go ahead and say it."

She gets a pained look on her face. "Maybe you should see where things go with Theo. You don't have to rush it—just let things progress naturally."

I shrug. "Maybe—"

Her shoulders relax, and she seems relieved that I'm not sprinting out the door to talk to Theo.

"It's so exhilarating when you start to have feelings for someone. Watching both you and Reagan is making me envious of that initial excitement."

I pull my knees to my chest. "What about Enrique?"

"Nah. I mean, I like him, but the magic just isn't there." She lets out a loud sigh. "Anyway, I think I'm going to take a hot bath." She stands up and stretches her arms over her head. "By the way, if you decide to cook anything, don't forget about the timer."

I cover my face with my hands. "I know. I promise I won't burn the house down."

"Good because I really love this place," she says with a laugh. "And maybe we should hang a warning sign out by the hammocks."

I groan. "You probably should hang a warning sign outside my room while you're at it."

She picks up her bag and heads to her bedroom.

I actually feel better after talking to Lila. I don't know what's going to happen between Theo and me, but it's a huge relief that Lila's not completely against it. The last thing I want is any tension around here.

It's probably a good thing that he's out of town. Now I won't wonder what he's doing or be tempted to rush over should any crisis arise. His absence gives me more time to really focus on other things—besides him.

Holy crap! My conversation with Theo distracted me from checking my messages every five seconds.

I dig in my bag for my phone, and sure enough there's a text waiting for me from the other realtor.

Offer accepted.

I let out a high-pitched scream as soon as I see it.

"Gabby, are you okay?" Lila shouts, running out of her bedroom in her bathrobe.

"They accepted the Sims' counter-offer."

Lila claps her hands together. "Awesome, congrats."

I quickly send a text to Danielle, giving her the exciting news.

Admittedly, I was worried. It's been a long time since I waited on the edge of my seat to hear about an offer. Back in Orlando, I'd reached a level in my career where I didn't stress about my sales. Building a brand from nothing is as challenging as I remember. This sale is exactly what I need to make my mark at Fun in the Sun Realty, and I hope it's only the beginning.

Chapter Eleven

"*C*ongratulations, Gabby," Elizabeth cheers.

I've been in Miami for three weeks, and I officially made my first sale.

Javier, Lila, and even Suzanna each hold up their champagne flutes to toast me. Despite trying to hold in the tears, I fail.

"Thank you so much," I say, getting choked up.

"Hold that thought," Elizabeth shouts. I wait as she scrolls through her phone. "Someone else wants to tell you congratulations."

My heart does a little flutter, and the image of Theo pops into my head.

She flips the phone around, and I see Nikki and Jason on the screen. That's all it takes to make the tears fall harder. There's a part of me that was hoping it was Theo, but I'm thrilled to see my brother and sister-in-law.

"Congrats, sis," Jason exclaims. "We knew you'd be lighting up that city in no time."

"Your brother is so cute," Lila whispers.

I make a face. Luckily Nikki doesn't hear her.

"Aw, I love seeing you guys. I miss you."

"We miss you, Gabs," Nikki says. "Keep up the great work. And tell Lizzy to be nice to you."

"I'm always nice," Elizabeth shouts, rolling her eyes.

As soon as Jason and Nikki are off the phone, I feel a little homesick. Even though I'm enjoying life here, there are aspects of Orlando that I miss. Namely, my family.

After our little celebration, everyone returns to their work and I finish up the paperwork for Danielle and Kevin's condo. They're also very interested in a gorgeous home in a nearby area called Parkland, so I'm hoping to get a purchase going for them very soon. Working with them has been a blessing, and I owe it all to Theo.

Thoughts of Theo really pull at my heart strings. The last time I saw him was our conversation across the lawn when he was leaving on his business trip. It's probably been good to have some space because I've buried myself in my work, and it's paying off. Although, there have been a few mornings I've woken up extra early and the first thoughts I had were of him swimming laps.

"Remember, you have the house to yourself tonight," Lila says, pulling her bag on her shoulder.

"Oh, yeah—tonight's the big charity event."

Lila finally decided to go with Jordan, whom I still haven't met. Apparently when she broke the news to Enrique, he didn't take it very well, and she learned an entire new vocabulary of Spanish words.

"Yep. And Reagan is going out for Kennedy's birthday."

I smile. "At Golden, of course."

Reagan frequents Dante's restaurant every chance she gets, so it's no surprise she suggested they celebrate her sister's birthday there.

"Don't worry, I'm not cooking tonight," I add. "I've already placed a to-go order."

Any time we discuss meals, the burnt pasta fiasco is mentioned.

"Thank goodness," she teases. "Okay, I'm off to my hair appointment. I'll see you later tonight."

After she leaves, I continue looking over the final contracts for the sale. It's been a while since I earned a commission like this one, and I'm thrilled. Between my move and months of emotional trauma, I burned through almost everything I had saved. I was one phone call away from asking my parents for money, which I haven't done in years.

Selling the Sims condo is helping me rebuild both my savings and my confidence.

I send Danielle a text before I leave the office.

Everything looks great. Thank you for giving me a chance to work with you.

I really like Danielle. You never know what you're going to get when you take on a new client. She's also given me two new leads, including Kevin's co-worker, so with those combined with the contacts Elizabeth shared with me, I'm feeling hopeful.

Moving to Miami has restored my faith in people. I left behind several strained relationships in Orlando, so these new friendships I'm forming have been such a blessing, and this includes Theo. Other than the unforgettable kisses we shared, it's safe to say that Theo and I are only friends. The issue is—as more time goes on, I realize I want to be more than that. I feel like I'm in a battle between what I think is good for me and what I really want.

After scarfing the salad and soup I ordered for dinner, I venture out onto the patio. I love this time of year in Florida. Although we don't get the traditional change of seasons, you can feel a difference when the weather changes, especially in the evenings. I still haven't gone near the hammocks, even though my sprained wrist is basically healed. I think someone should be with me before I attempt them again.

The sun hasn't set yet, but it's starting to cool off from the heat of the day. I kick off my flip-flops, sit on the edge of the pool, and dip my feet in. When I glance over at Theo's house, I can't help but wonder if he's home from his trip yet.

All of a sudden, a wasp starts buzzing around, landing on top of the water near my feet. The only thing I'm more scared of than parallel parking is wasps. I quickly hop out of the pool just in case I need to make a quick getaway. Thankfully, the hideous insect lurks around for a few seconds and then flies away.

I breathe a sigh of relief as I go to sit down again, when the evil creature returns, heading straight toward me. I'm in such a panic that I step to the side and lose my balance, screaming as I fall into the pool.

The warm water engulfs me, and when I lift my head out of the water, I see Theo dropping to his knees next to the pool. He reaches his hand out and helps me out of the water. As soon as I'm out, he looks down at my clothes and gives me a confused look.

Ugh. It's just another typical day in my life and another moment of pure humiliation in front of Theo.

"I fell into the pool."

The corners of his mouth curl up, and he bursts out laughing.

I try to act like I'm annoyed, but his laughter is contagious.

After he runs inside my house to get me a towel, he asks me what happened. I tell him about the wasp and losing my balance.

"So, you were running from a wasp?"

"Yep."

He shakes his head as he continues to laugh.

"What are you doing here?" I ask.

I'm not surprised Theo showed up, but I'm so happy he did.

"I was outside heating up the grill to make some chicken when I heard you scream."

Of course he did.

"And you came to my rescue—again."

He shrugs nonchalantly. "You weren't drowning."

"No, but you were here when I needed you." I pull the towel tightly around me.

He rubs his forehead. "For some reason I have a hard time staying away."

There's a familiar flutter in my chest. Why am I fighting this? There are obvious forces at work that continue to put us in each other's paths.

"Gabby, I've been thinking—"

I hold up my hand to stop him. "Me too, but I'd really love to get out of these wet clothes."

He nods. "Will you come over after you're done—just to talk?"

Yes! Yes! Yes!

"I'd like that."

I watch as he saunters back to his house, and I rush inside to dry off and get changed. I'm a ball of nerves as I think about the conversation we're about to have. My main focus has to be my career but staying away from Theo doesn't seem to be working out for me.

My mind is racing as I blow-dry my hair. Theo is back, and for some reason the universe has thrust us back together once again—maybe this is another sign telling me not to fight the inevitable. I try to relax before I put my makeup on. A shaky hand isn't good when mascara is involved. I change into a pair of jeans and a V-neck pink shirt. It's time for Theo to see me dressed like a functioning human being. And yes, I may be overdoing it, but I don't care. It feels like I'm doing everything backwards when it comes to Theo. Shockingly, he hasn't run away yet. And that might be the answer I'm looking for.

After one more look in the mirror, I take a deep breath and head next door. Even though I've always cut through the backyards, I decide to go to his front door and ring the bell.

When he answers the door, he looks me up and down. "Wow."

I hold my arms up. "This is how I look when I'm not in my pajamas, or dripping wet, or crying my eyes out."

He presses his lips together. "Hmm … I do like the cute PJs and the bedhead. But I'm not complaining."

He holds the door open wider, and I step inside. "I expected you to come to the back door."

I laugh. "Yeah, I figured I'd try to be as normal as possible tonight."

"Normal is overrated."

"That's a good thing," I say.

I follow Theo to his kitchen, where I'm met with a savory aroma.

"Would you like some grilled chicken?" he asks. "I should warn you, it's not as good as my omelets."

I shake my head. "I already ate, but I'd love a glass of wine."

I'll take all the liquid courage I can get right now.

After pouring me a glass, we talk about his trip while he eats, and then I tell him about selling Danielle and Kevin's condo.

"Congratulations." He holds up his wine glass, and I touch mine to it.

"I never would've had the opportunity if it weren't for you."

He shakes his head. "I only gave a recommendation. You made the sale."

"Your recommendation was huge for me. I was pretty close to going broke and surviving on Lucky Charms alone."

He laughs. "There are worse things."

We both get quiet as we sip our wine.

"So, how is it living with my good friend Lila?"

I giggle. "Believe it or not—it's great. In fact, I think I have her closer to considering a truce with you."

He throws his head back. "Now that's funny."

"I'm dead serious."

He puts his glass down. "Well, I hope she means it because I really enjoy spending time with you."

My heart starts to race.

"Why don't we go sit down," he suggests.

He takes my hand and leads me to the couch. We sit next to each other, and he stretches his arm along the top of the couch behind me. Having him close to me feels so good.

"I was actually wondering if part of the reason you stepped back was because of Lila."

Ugh. I knew this was going to come up, and I'm determined to be honest with him.

His eyes lock on mine as he waits for me to say something.

"Lila had nothing to do with it." I clear my throat as I prepare to tell him everything.

"When I moved here my plan was to put everything I had into focusing on my career. I never expected to meet you and have a connection so quickly," I say, twisting my fingers.

"Neither did I," he says softly. "The truth is that the second you fell out of the hammock, I was hooked."

Hooked? I definitely didn't expect him to say that.

"I just don't know if I'm ready to open my heart again—I'm scared."

He squeezes my hand. "So am I. In fact, there's something I want to share with you."

My heart begins to beat faster. I wonder if this is what Danielle was talking about.

"After my mom passed away, I bounced from one relationship to another until I met my ex-girlfriend. We were together almost a year, and I finally thought I was ready to settle down." He rubs the back of his neck nervously. "We talked about marriage a lot. And then one day out of the blue, I woke up in a panic, and I ended our relationship that day."

He gets a pained look on his face. "Naturally she took it hard, but I couldn't commit when I wasn't in the right state of mind."

It's obvious that Theo carries a lot of regret for hurting his ex-girlfriend.

"At least you didn't sleep with her best friend," I point out.

"Not a chance. I'd never do something like that," he assures me. "Anyway, the reason I'm telling you this is because I want to be honest. I was nervous about it because you've dealt with more than your share of dishonesty."

Theo pushes my hair behind my ear, and his touch sends tingles through my body. I'm still afraid of getting hurt again, but I think I'm more afraid of walking away from the feeling I have sitting here with him.

"What are you thinking about?" he asks a few seconds later.

I look him directly in the eyes. "Honestly, I was thinking about how much I love being here with you, and I was remembering the morning you made me breakfast."

He grins. "I've thought about that morning a lot too and ..."

"And what?"

"And I hope we'll be watching a lot more Miami sunrises together. How does that sound?"

My heart practically beats out of my chest.

"I think it sounds perfect."

He doesn't waste any time gently taking my face in his hands and kissing me. His kiss is slow and meaningful, and I allow myself to savor every second of it. I know this is the first of many more evenings together, and I'm okay with that. I'm determined more than ever to embrace every aspect of life here in Miami and with Theo.

A few hours later, Theo and I walk hand in hand back to my house.

"Shall we continue this tomorrow?" he asks, wrapping his hands around my waist. "Would you prefer to meet at the wall or at the hammock?"

I laugh. "Either one works for me."

He leans down and kisses me on the forehead. "Sweet dreams, Gabby."

"Good night."

I quietly sneak back into the house, even though I'm not sure if my roommates are even home yet.

When I finally crawl into bed, I still have a smile on my face. As I stare at the ceiling, I think about all the possibilities the future holds. I know some days are going to be more difficult than others, but in this very moment I'm content, which is good enough for me.

"Miami, you're everything I dreamed of and more. Thanks for the friendship ... and the love."

The End

Check out the other books in the Thankful series! Thanks for the Memories and Thanks for the Friendship are now available!

Thanks for the Memories Now Available

Buy the second book in the Thankful Series on Amazon or read with your KindleUnlimited membership!

A new beginning leads to a second-chance at romance.

Done with the frigid northern winters, Reagan Westbourne has an easy solution—move to Miami. It makes total sense. She can even live with her sister. But after a few months of enduring her quirky sibling's newlywed bliss, Reagan is ready to spread her wings and move out. Life with two fun roommates and a promising job completes the picture for Reagan. Almost.

When Reagan's old college friend, Dante, opens a new restaurant in Miami, the past mixes with the present. After all, he's the only man Reagan's ever had feelings for. And it seems the attraction might just be mutual. Yet when their paths finally seem to align, old and new friends enter the picture, leaving Reagan unsure of her feelings.

Could this second-chance be the answer, or is it time to leave the memories in the past?

Dear Reader

I hope you enjoyed *Thanks for the Love*. Please take a few minutes to leave a review on Amazon. Check out Thanks for the Memories, the next book in the Thankful series.

Love my books? Join my Facebook reader group. Interested in a free book? Click here.

Visit my website for updates, and stay tuned for my next book coming soon.

AuthorMelissaBaldwin.com

About the Author

USA Today bestselling author Melissa Baldwin is a planner-obsessed Disney fan who still watches Beverly Hills 90210 reruns and General Hospital.

She's a wife, mother, and journal keeper, who finally decided to write the book she talked about for years. She took her dream to the next level, and is now an award-winning, bestselling author of twenty-one Romantic Comedy and Cozy Mystery novels and novellas. Melissa writes about charming, ambitious, and real women, and she considers these leading ladies to be part of her tribe.

When she isn't deep in the writing zone, this multitasking master organizer keeps busy by spending time with her family, chauffeuring her daughter, traveling, attempting yoga poses, and going on rides at Disney World.

Visit authormelissabaldwin.com to sign up for her newsletter.

Printed in Great Britain
by Amazon